MW01206417

Carried By the Eastern

Wind

By Erin Pirani

Carried by the Eastern Wind

GENRE: HISTORICAL ROMANCE

Carried By the Eastern Wind

Copyright © 2017 by Erin Pirani

Cover Design by Winter Bayne

First Publication: August 2017

Published by Erin Pirani ~ United States of America

ISBN-13:9781975829193
ISBN-10:1975829190

I want to dedicate this story to my husband, who has been my rock, support, and my inspiration throughout this entire adventure called marriage.

He was dark, dangerous, and secretive…

Lieutenant Ali Raza oversees a nominal company of soldiers—the Indian infantry. They are battling for control of the textile trade over the British government. To the Crown, it's an act of rebellion; to Ali it's an act of independence. After a brief victory, Ali is brutally attacked and left to die in the harsh desert. Thought to have deserted his post, Ali is discharged from the army and humiliated. Determined to find his assailant and clear his name, Ali finds his saving grace in the arms of the beautiful seamstress, Charmaine Radcliff, after a daring escape. The pair is thrust into a whirlwind romance, and a fight for both of their lives. She was beautiful, irresistible, and downright distracting…

Charmaine Radcliff is a beautiful, independent, and headstrong woman who never dreamed that she would be in the arms of a handsome Indian Army officer with a dangerous secret. When she is kidnapped for uncovering a drug ring, Ali comes to her rescue. In exchange for saving her life, she aids him in finding his assailant while trying to uncover his secret. However, she never expected love would be part of the deal.

Chapter 1

Thar Desert, India 1910

The scorching sun beat down on the Thar Desert with such ferocity, making it hotter than usual. Sweat dripped like a stream from the men's foreheads. The heavy wool uniforms they wore didn't help, but the desert heat didn't bother Lieutenant Ali Raza. He'd disowned all forms of traditional military dress, wearing only a simple white button-down shirt that accentuated his stature. Fawn-colored breeches and knee-high black boots completed his ensemble. He found it adequate for a dangerous excursion such as this. His superiors scorned him for his lack of conduct. That mattered little to Ali. What did bother him was something he could not put his finger on. Something was amiss; he could feel it in his bones. He just needed to find out what.

Ali dragged his men out to the desert because he knew they could handle it. He and his companions had lived in this harsh environment all their lives. But the British Cavalry could not tolerate the severity of the desert and all its hidden dangers. In fact, the only reason the British were in this godforsaken place was because of the textile trade route. By controlling that, they would be the most formidable force in the trading industry. But Ali would die fighting before he let that happen. Luckily, he was an excellent marksman. He eyed his company one final time, securing every position, withholding the order to fire until the last possible minute.

When he saw one of the soldiers was too shocked to act, he snatched the Ottoman Rifle from the terrified soldier and aimed to fire at the oncoming enemy.

The thunder of the oncoming cavalry grew closer.

"Ready, men! Reload, and arm yourselves!" Ali ordered. On command, the soldiers drew their Ottoman Rifles into position. The sound of triggers clicked in unison, ready to fire on the enemy once more.

"Aim!"

"FIRE!" The first round of shots rang out. A few soldiers fell, but not enough to do any damage. Torrents of smoke surrounded the regiment, yet the soldiers endured and continued to fire on the oncoming enemy.

Damn. They were too close.

"Get ready!"

The men reloaded their weapons as swiftly as they could. The lines shifted for the second round of attacks.

"Fire!" came the second command. Gunfire exploded.

Success. The shots tore into the oncoming soldiers, rending flesh, cutting the enemy down into the desert sands in an instant. The dying screams vibrated miles away, but the problem remained. The British were drawing closer every second. Ali needed to prepare his men for the battle that was about to ensue.

"Ready yourselves, men! We fight hand to hand. If we die, we die with honor!"

The resounding ring of steel echoed in the arid air as the men drew their swords. Ali followed suit by releasing his two long knives from his belt. He stood poised, ready to pounce.

"Here they come," Ali said to himself.

One by one, the enemy came to him. His knives moved as swift as lightning. Everything blurred as he knocked the soldiers off their horses. He took caution not to miss a single one. Then it was over. The enemy had fallen. As the remaining British retreated, Ali's senses continued to tingle. He continued to remain poised, still on his guard, scanning his surroundings. The sound of running echoed off the sand, closing in behind him.

He straightened his stance. Maneuvering his left leg, he tripped the lowly officer who was coming towards him. The man picked himself up when Ali kicked him to the ground once again, crossing both his knives over the soldier's throat. A threatening tone laced his voice.

"Leave this place and never return, or I will not hesitate to kill you."

The man nodded his head, acknowledging the threat. Ali released his knives, rising from the timorous soldier. The man did not delay any further to join the rest of his regiment, which was quickly retreating.

Sheathing his knives, Ali shook his head, regretting the words that had escaped his lips. The battle had ended. For now. The final toll was fifteen. Fifteen of Ali's men had died, nothing in comparison to the British who had lost more than twenty-five of their soldiers. His men were best the Indian Army had to offer, a senseless waste because of this battle. At least they were safe for now; who knew what the scum planned next?

Before he'd died, Ali's father had taught him the art of combat. When Ali was old enough he joined the ranks of

3

Indian soldiers, and trained with his peers. Years had passed since then. And Ali had perfected the art, building his skills and readying for a life of fighting. Since he was unusually tall and muscular, versus the average five-foot-seven inches of most Indian men, it seemed the only life tailored for a man like him.

It was a wonder he managed to keep his compassion and, somehow, his sanity. For twenty-four years he had lived alone, preferring his own company to that of others.

When he left home, Ali promised his mother he would make it home one day; proving himself worthy to marry into a good family, as was expected of him. Not for love of course, but for respect. And to give his mother a proper life with a higher status. Till then, he would serve in the military in the hopes that the day would soon arrive.

Ali banished the thought to survey the scene before him, identifying the injured and speaking a few words to the few who could walk. The field reeked of the sickening odor of blood and gunpowder. No matter how long he had been in the army, he would never get used to the stench.

"Tend to the injured." He gave the orders to the soldiers who lingered before striding back to his tent.

As instructed, the remaining soldiers assisted one another. Taking a cleaning cloth from his pocket, Ali wiped the blood from his long knife in one swift motion. His second in command and longtime family friend, Rajesh Suneel, joined his side. He slapped Ali on the back when he approached.

"We sure showed them! Those dogs will think twice before they come up against us again."

"Our men fought with valor, but we should regroup and come up with a second plan of attack. So we don't become surprised." Ali spoke with calm as Rajesh placed a water skin in his hands.

"*Koi masla nahi*. No worries. Like I said, they won't be coming back. Trust me." A devilish smile crossed Rajesh's lips.

"You never know." Ali took a long drink from the water skin.

"Our men are the best; there's no way the British will return. *Chalo*. Let's go," he said, signaling with a nod of his head to walk.

"We need to report to General Moshin before we plan anything else. Not to mention getting our men out of this heat before anything else happens," Ali said as he put a hand on his forehead. He began to feel dizzy, placing his other hand on his friend's shoulder to walk.

"The men will be fine; we'll report to General Moshin. Oh, one more thing…"

Rajesh's voice was becoming distant, and inaudible. "Say again? The heat—?" He could see his lips moving, yet he still could not hear the words his comrade was saying. Ali shook his head to clear his thoughts, but it was futile because his world went black.

Chapter 2

He could hear the grumbling of camels. Was he dreaming, or going mad? For some reason, he couldn't wake up, no matter how hard he tried. His eyes felt as if they were sewn shut. And his head was swimming. He was so hot. That was unusual, as he was never hot.

He could hear several whispering voices.

"Over here."

"Who is he?"

"Is he dead?

Then quiet. Nothing at all. He slipped back into unconsciousness.

Ali was struggling to open his eyes. *Am I still in the desert?*

Everything was spinning. A foggy haze clouded his senses. His mouth was parched, like the sand, and his body too weak to move. He could tell he was in a soft bed by the way the silk felt against his skin.

Old, masculine hands reached over and blotted his forehead. The water was refreshing, a cool contrast against the burning that resonated in his body.

"You must get some rest my son; you are still far too weak."

"Where am I?" he managed to whisper through cracked lips. His eyes burned, not to mention the persistent hammering in his head. Experienced hands reached under his neck to pull his head up, allowing a trickle of water into his parched mouth.

"You are safe. Now sleep; we'll talk more when you are strong enough," the kind voice urged.

Ali obeyed the voice that spoke. Although he couldn't see, he could feel the wash towel over his eyes as he fell back into a comatose-like sleep.

Candlelight illuminated the tent when Ali woke that evening. The temperature had cooled to a comfortable enough degree that Ali, clad only in his breeches, had his top half exposed.

The chill of the night drew out the day's heat from his body. His white button- down shirt was discarded, neatly folded on the assortment of decorative pillows on the other side of the tent.

He could open his eyes now, slowly, despite the dull ache in his head. He sat up in bed, looking around for the old hands that tended to him earlier. The shadow of a large man lingered in the threshold of the tent.

Judging by the way he looked the man was in his sixties, with a medium white beard, thick white hair, and soft brown eyes. He was around five-foot-nine and rotund; only an inch taller than Ali. The man's clothing was bright red and yellow. His face full of cheer.

"Ahhh, you are awake at last," his voice boomed.

The old man brought Ali a water skin, along with a plate of flat bread, dates, and oranges located on the opposite end of the room. Ali hesitated as he placed the opening to his lips. After a moment, he had decided it was safe. Tilting the skin to his mouth he drank with gusto. The man set the plate on the bed next to Ali as he pulled up a stool of red velvet to sit by the bedside.

"You must eat and regain your strength; you were almost lost to us when we found you."

"What happened? How did I come to be here? And who are you?"

The old man chuckled. Mehdi then placed some *naan*, or flat bread, into his lap.

"So many questions, all will have answers in time. For now, you may call me Mehdi, or Uncle. I am one of the elders of our tribe, although we do not stay in one place for long."

"You are nomads then?"

The older man released a soft chuckle to the response.

"One would call us that. Yes."

Ali took some of the flat bread, broke it off, and began eating. He gave a nod to show his appreciation and thanks.

"We know not how you came to the desert, but you are welcome whatever the case may be. You were unconscious for hours; on the brink of death. By the grace of God we were able to get to you in time," Mehdi explained as he handed the wearied Ali more *naan.*

"God has failed me in this place," Ali replied, full of spite.

9

"Never give up, my son. If He brought you into it, He will see you out of it. Do you remember anything before all this? What is your name?"

"My name is Lieutenant Ali Raza. We were fighting off the cursed English in the Thar Desert. The East India Trade Company wants complete control over the textile industry. It was a good fight, but it ended much too soon; it is too suspicious. The English did not put up as much of a fight as I had expected. I was talking to my Second Lieutenant, Rajesh Suneel, about our victory. After that, I don't remember."

Mehdi spoke with caution. "We know not how you became unresponsive in the desert. Do you think someone may have brought you here…because they wanted you dead?"

"I believe that may be the case. I may have an idea of who it was. Although, I fear accusing the wrong man."

"Perhaps so. We did find these items next to you when we rescued you." Turning in the stool, he lifted a red silk cloth from next to the bed to place it in Ali's lap. "They may help you identify the one who is responsible." Ali unwrapped the cloth that was on his lap. Inside lay a slender dagger. Handcrafted dark wood colored the hilt. Two golden flower emblems were on opposite ends of the handle. Small golden flowers were painted down to metal tip.

The second item was a worn piece of paper. The wax seal bore a three-headed lion, accompanied by two crossing swords underneath.

"The crest of the Army," Ali said aloud. Reluctant to take the paper, he didn't want to know what it contained.

With a swift motion, Ali broke the wax. It was exactly what he feared.

Addressed to Lt. Ali Raza

On Suspicion of Desertion. Lt. Raza. On the 7th day of February, Year 1910. Due to failure to return to base, to give a full report on the English to your superior officers. Because of this, you are hereby discharged from the Indian Army. Please report to base to await further action.

Sincerely,

Major General Moshin Sher.

Ali put the paper down, leaned his head back, and released a breath of frustration.

"This makes no sense. Why would General Moshin discharge me without further evidence? Unless..." Ali studied the missive more closely.

Mehdi put an arm on his shoulder and spoke. "If you should need any help from any of my people or myself, do not hesitate to ask."

"Thank you, Uncle."

Mehdi then leaned over to see the letter in Ali's hand.

"May I see that letter?"

Ali gave the paper to Mehdi. After a few minutes, he spoke.

"This paper, it's not from here." He ran his thumb over the smooth surface.

"Meaning?"

"You do not see." Mehdi handed back the letter to Ali to see for himself.

Ali put a finger over wax bumps that were on the paper.

"I don't see what you see."

"The writing on the paper. As you said, it doesn't make sense. It's not what it seems. But…" Mehdi examined the fiber content

Mehdi took a final glance before Ali whisked the paper away.

The elder called for a servant by the name of Rahman.

A few minutes later, the man he'd called for came in. Mehdi spoke, thus giving the letter to the smaller man so he could examine it. Several minutes of silence dragged on. The two men were discussing in a language that was not familiar to Ali. Ali knew that many various dialects resided in these parts. Although Ali was skilled in only a few of these languages, translating this particular one had not been easy.

The man nodded, which gave him his guarantee. The two men, when finished with the conversation, turned to Ali.

"It's confirmed, what we had first thought. The letter isn't what it appears; it could have come from the English." Mehdi gestured his right hand to his comrade. "Rahman is an expert in such things."

It was Ali's turn to speak. "You speak in riddles, sir. We do trade with Europe, and it's not uncommon for English goods to come into our hands." He paused for a moment before speaking again.

"What do you suggest I do?"

"You could go to England. There you could find out who has written this letter. Find out as much as you can. As for the letter itself, I cannot tell who has written it. That, you need to discover for yourself."

Ali turned his head, calculating his next move.

"Get some sleep; you do not have to decide everything tonight. Mayhap your answer will come in the morning." Ali then turned to Mehdi and nodded his head in answer.

Mehdi and Rahman exited the tent to give Ali some privacy to sleep.

"Why did you not tell him?"

"Because he needs to find the answer on his own. I have a premonition he will have the answers he is looking for in England. And once he learns those answers, he will find his battle skills of little use."

Day by day, his strength returned. He slept during the day, then at night he would dine along with additional members of Mehdi's small tribe. Ali learned much from Mehdi's advice.

When Ali rose early one warm morning, he had made up his mind that it was time for him to go.

Mehdi was right: a much-needed rest was the answer. He was able to dress with no trouble, buttoning his white shirt and breeches.

Walking towards a large red canopy, he spotted Mehdi sticking out like a beacon in the ink-black night. He passed a small group of women wearing similar robes as the men, giggling and whispering. He gave a curt nod, acknowledging their presence as a gentleman would. They continued to whisper as he continued to walk. It wasn't unusual for women to fawn over him; he had been told many times that he was a handsome specimen. Although he never believed it to be so.

Mehdi saw Ali from a distance from his shaded tent. He peered up from the maps that he was researching with several other men. When he approached the humble man, he spoke in his usual booming voice.

"You look as good as new, my boy. Have you decided what you will do now?" asked Mehdi.

"I have decided to travel across the seas to Europe, as you have suggested. Perhaps, on the way there, I will find the answers I am searching for."

"Will you stay one more night, to further detail your plans? You may travel with my tribe as we journey west."

"I wish I could, Uncle, but I am pressed for time. I must find out who tried to kill me, and stop him before he goes any further."

"I understand. Will you not report to your camp to explain what happened? You could clear this entire mess."

"Uncle, if I return to my base camp, I will become reprimanded. Then I will never the answers I'm looking for."

"I see." Mehdi gave a quizzical response as he stroked his cloud-white beard.

"One more thing, Uncle." Ali took the dagger they retrieved from the desert, and handed it to Mehdi. "This dagger you found with me. Do you know anything of it? I haven't been myself the last several nights, so I neglected to ask."

Mehdi took the dagger from Ali's hand to study it. "This dagger you have found is not from this region; it seems to be similar to the Kindjal family from Turkey. Ottoman, to be precise."

Just as I thought. Our rifles are of Ottoman make…he had it custom made, possibly before we left. "Then my suspicions of who possessed it are growing stronger. And my mission has become more urgent than I had expected. Thank you for everything, Uncle; I do not know how I can show my gratitude for your kindness you have shown me." Ali clasped hands with the old man.

"Think nothing of it," Mehdi exchanged to him. "I hope you find what you are searching for."

Hours later, Ali finished gathering the rest of his belongings. Positioning the satchel around his torso, he readied himself for the long journey ahead. Walking from the taupe-colored tent that had been his home for the last few weeks, Ali bid Medhi and the others a fond farewell. He took the food the nomad tribe had given him, a water-skin, and extra coins if he should need it. It took Ali two full weeks to reach the city of Kolachi. He slept during the day in rock shelters, and traveled at night to avoid heat exposure. His water supply was depleted by the time he reached the city port.

If he had found an oasis, perhaps he could have prolonged the supply. Due to the circumstances, he needed to make do with what he had.

The dock was a tumult of activity, people boarding and departing from the many of the different ships. Merchants selling their wares, the faint scent of sandalwood, spices, and burning wood permeated the air. This was overpowered by the stench of camel entrails.

Ali could hardly think with all the shouting between the businessmen, enticing customers to purchase the many different merchandise. It was a wonder he was able to make it through the throngs of people without the crowd swallowing him up.

I should replenish my supplies.

When Ali entered the shop, he gave the water skin to the man behind the counter to have it filled. He turned to lean on the edge of the worn wood counter. He spied a man of similar height, wearing a white turban. The only difference was the flash of blue eyes as he walked out the door. He stood straight and tall, on his guard.

"Rajesh? No, it can't be."

The clerk turned to face Ali, to hand him the water skin. Ali snatched it out of his hand, quick as lightning, throwing two coins onto the counter top before he ran from the shop to catch up with the mysterious blue-eyed man.

When Ali reached the outside, he was gone. His point of interest was swallowed up by the bustling crowd. Leaning against the frame of the door, Ali shook his head to clear his thoughts. He made his descent into the crowd once more to find his ship to take him across the sea.

Chapter 3

Acton Suburb, London, England, 1910

Charmaine Radcliff stood by the window of her second-story bedroom. She was dressed in a floor-length white lace petticoat and corset, her cream shawl wrapped snug around her shoulders. Before her, women strolled about the busy streets of Acton, and children skipped alongside their mothers while holding onto their hands. Several businessmen barreled on by.

Her long auburn hair flowed down her back as she turned her face toward the sunshine. She closed her eyes and inhaled deeply. The essence of lavender perfume wafted throughout the space, calming her mind. A ghost of a smile appeared on her face when she spoke aloud to herself. "Soon, I will enjoy my time like others do. Once Papa is out of debt, we will not have to worry *about anything.*"

As Charmaine continued to daydream about the future, a sudden shiver trailed up her spine. Opening her eyes with a jolt, her hands roamed up and down her arms to warm herself from the sudden chill that wracked her body.

Where did that come from?

Wrapping her shawl tighter around herself, Charmaine looked around the empty room to see what could have caused it.

19

The silence was her only answer. She touched a hand to the chestnut framed window.

Locked. Just as she'd thought. *Odd.*

To suppress the oncoming anxiety that gripped her body, Charmaine closed her eyes and inhaled with slow, rhythmic breaths. When the tremor had passed, Charmaine was able to gather her wits and breathe with calm again.

Charmaine pivoted away from the window, striding across the hardwood floor, and tossed the cream lace shawl onto the foot of her bed. She opened up the small chestnut wardrobe, only to be disappointed to find a dismal selection of gowns available.

Her papa had wanted her to have an education suitable for a lady. Thus, vestments to enlighten that aspect of her life. Unfortunately, the education bestowed upon her never went into use. Charmaine had no choice to but to sell most of her beautiful gowns to help keep herself and her papa afloat. After the shipping business went into decline, no gentlemen came to call. Over time, Arthur Radcliff had tried in vain to salvage whatever remained of his business. Alas, it wasn't meant to be, and ruination befell the Radcliff name. At the age of twenty-two, it seemed there was no other option for Charmaine now but to work, and accept the life of a spinster.

Shaking her head to dismiss a small tear drop that escaped her eye, she reached for the violet gown with a square lace neck. Four gold buttons lay in a uniform line, which divided the square bodice. A beautiful silk white sash attached to the front wrapped around her waist, enhancing the beautiful purple color. After dressing, she placed a few pins to secure the bun centered at the nape of her neck. A black ribbon tied around the crown of her head, she adjusted her head piece as she took one last look in the full-length mirror. A blank stare reflected back at her, a shell of her former self.

Charmaine noticed a metal object reflecting light from the sun, so she whirled around and stalked to the open davenport. A tarnished silver oval picture frame, which sat on the writing desk, rattled her. "William." The bitterness she expressed surprised her. Even though time had passed, the wound was still fresh. She forced open the top desk drawer, she tossed the photo inside, and slammed the drawer shut.

Out of sight, out of mind.

Running her hands down her dress, she brushed out any remaining wrinkles. "Right, this will have to do," she murmured aloud.

The wood creaked with each step as Charmaine crept down the stairs. She spied her father. Arthur Radcliff stared out the bay window lost in his thoughts, puffing his pipe in one hand, the other in his pocket. Charmaine noticed his melancholy mood, a ghost of his former self, staring out from within. Given his current state, she knew there was nothing that could be done at this point. So, Charmaine left him to glower out the window as she left for Mrs. Henrietta's shop.

~*~*~

Early evening had fallen when Charmaine finished the remaining work at Mrs. Henrietta's seamstress shop. She didn't mind assisting Henrietta Flint, and every night Henrietta trusted Charmaine to close the shop. A certain sense of pride swelled within as she completed her responsibilities. It wasn't the most prestigious shop; on the contrary, it was a quaint, modest establishment nestled in the back streets of London.

If Mama hadn't left years ago, we wouldn't be in this mess.

After all the pain and embarrassment, Charmaine needed to do what she could to keep her and Papa afloat. She had tried her best to take care of what was left of her family throughout the years after, but nothing seemed to work.

The occurrence feels like it was only yesterday, and Papa has never been the same since.

Since then, Charmaine had been left alone to fend for herself, thus destroying Papa's hopes of a successful marriage for her in the process. Distraught, Charmaine had been about to give up on everything until her papa suggested that she reach out to Henrietta. It wasn't in Charmaine's nature to plead, but she saw no other choice in the matter. Henrietta had the heart to take her in after every other employer had turned her out. In fact, the only reason she was able to get the job as Henrietta's assistant was because of her mother, who had known Henrietta since childhood.

Charmaine pondered the status of her hideous reputation as she opened the cash register, her fingertips caressing the paper notes. Immediately her mind addressed the unopened stack of letters stacked in a dusty corner of the writing desk. Charmaine had her qualms about her mother; she had so many questions that needed answering, but she hadn't mustered up the courage to read a single letter postmarked to her.

She wasn't ready to forgive, not yet. Her mother destroyed any chance of making a suitable life for her, leaving her destitute. Because of this, no respectable man in this city would even look at her anymore.

William Tate also saw to that as well when he stole whatever finances her father had left, thus tarnishing her reputation along with it.

He'll get his comeuppance soon enough. She stopped counting the money when she lost her train of thought.

Maybe Mrs. Henrietta will allow me to take over one day.

She looked up, turning her attention to the large display window where some of her creations stood. Creations Charmaine made with her own hands; elegant, floor-length gowns adorned life-size mannequins. Beautiful bright hues, lace, buttons, and ribbon wrapped around the mannequins' slender forms, transforming many of her imaginings into reality. Charmaine created these works of art for society ladies, although she couldn't help but dream to wear one of those

23

gowns one day. How wonderful to one day walk in the shoes of those elite women who attended the fancy parties, wear those exquisite ensembles, dance till dawn, and mingle with the crème-de-la-crème of society.

One can only dream.

She placed the remaining notes into a bag, while pushing the cash drawer shut with her other hand. Charmaine formed her hands into a ball, blowing warm air into the small opening a few times. The temperature had cooled, as it often did in springtime in London, yet Charmaine was just as cold in the shop as she was in her room earlier that morning. She stood in a full upright position when she placed the palms of her hands on her neck, further guarding herself against the chill.

Strolling to the far end of the room, with the money bag tucked in the crook of her arm, Charmaine removed her hands from her lips and dimmed the oil lamp. She paused at the sound of unfamiliar voices coming from the back office, and pivoted in one, fluid motion. Tiptoeing to the back room, she went to investigate.

The hardwood squeaked under her feet. Charmaine did her best to be quiet, but the narrow hall seemed to have no end. After a few minutes of agonizing quiet, the journey was a success. There at the end of the hall was a white paneled door, which stood ajar.

That's where the voices are coming from.

Crouching down to peek through the crack of the door, Charmaine could see Henrietta's office, and two men conversing. She squinted her eyes for a better look. *Drat*—their backs were turned.

"Is this some kind of a joke, Henrietta?" came an angry male voice.

"This is no scam, gentlemen; you will get your payments in time as long as long as I get what is mine."

Mrs. Henrietta's voice? No, it couldn't be true. No. Charmaine was stunned.

"We couldn't sell this opium even if it was led to believe it to be the best," one of the men said, holding up a packet. He slammed it onto the table, a white dust cloud forming in the middle of the oak desk where Henrietta Flint sat. A taller, broader man stood behind her. His black bowler hat was pulled down over his eyes.

"We had a deal, Flint!" the brown-haired man hissed.

"We still have one case left to sell, gentlemen. You will get the money you require." Henrietta's voice echoed.

"Opium," Charmaine whispered to herself. *Mrs. Henrietta is smuggling opium out of the shop.* She couldn't believe it. There sat her boss—a woman she trusted—at her desk, fingers folded together, talking with strange men about opium.

All went quiet.

I have to tell the police.

Charmaine stood straight as she backed away from the door, her heart pounding in her chest as she continued farther and farther away, until her back met the wall. Just then, the door flew open, and a blond-haired man covered the entrance.

"It seems we have a mouse," he breathed out.

"Don't let her escape," Henrietta shouted, rising from her desk. Charmaine's first instinct was to run, but she was frozen in fear.

The man with the brown hair came up next to her, blocking her escape. The money purse clutched under her arm fell to the floor as the blond man pushed Charmaine into the office. He shoved her into a chair, facing Henrietta.

"Mrs. Henrietta—what's—Why?!" Charmaine managed to stammer out as bile rose from her stomach.

Henrietta turned away from her. "These are hard times, and things have changed; making clothing can't be the only source of income. My funds are dwindling and women's clothing is being mass produced faster than I can sew. Thus, my creativity, my work of art, is becoming extinct." Henrietta sucked in a breath before beginning again. "And being a divorcee does not bode well for me. My shop is failing, and in lieu of certain events, I had to make do with what I had. A partner for this trade became a necessity." Charmaine turned her head to the broad-shouldered man; his ominous blue eyes peered out from beneath the round bowler hat. Now that she had a closer look at him, he was much darker than the other two. His dark skin reminded her of toffee.

"I don't understand. I thought we were doing so well," Charmaine managed to squeak out.

Henrietta walked towards Charmaine, lifting her chin as she spoke. "This is a man's world, my dear angel, and it's sorely unfair for women. After my divorce, I was left with nothing to my name and stained reputation to go with it. I needed to do what I had to, to stay ahead. And with this money I have earned from selling the opium, I'll have more than enough to keep this shop going. Although..." Henrietta stopped in mid-sentence, clasping her aged hands to her abdomen.

"Although, what?" Charmaine answered, fearing the answer more than the question.

"You could join me. If you keep quiet about what happened here, you can have a percentage of the earnings."

"You're mad if you think I'll accept such an offer," Charmaine spat out.

"Unfortunate, that," Henrietta muttered to herself. "Well, we can't have you tell the police of our little discovery either." She faced the brown-haired man. "Jasper. Tell the driver to bring the carriage around." Jasper nodded, then left the room. "Such a pity, too. You were such a sweet thing, so much like your mother." Henrietta's French accent slipped through.

"What are you going to do with me?" Charmaine cried.

Ignoring her, Henrietta snapped her fingers. "Oliver, take Jonathan and Jasper with you. Do what you like with her, just make sure she is unable to breathe a word to the Bobbies."

Jonathan and Oliver griped Charmaine's arms, hoisting her from the chair; her face blanched from fear as the two men dragged her from the office. Henrietta walked into to the hall where Charmaine had dropped the money purse, and smiled.

Chapter 4

A jet-black carriage lay in wait in the back alley. In the driver's seat, dressed all in black, she saw the coachman. The mystery man glanced in her direction; their eyes locked for a brief moment before he turned away. His dark eyes were the only thing visible beneath a worn black top hat. While struggling in Jasper's iron-like grip, Charmaine searched for another means of escape, but Jasper forced her into the horse-drawn carriage before she could enact her plan. Once secured, Jasper then dashed atop to seat himself next to the driver. With Oliver sitting at her left, any hope Charmaine had of escape died.

~*~

Ali, perched atop the driver's seat, was disguised in a black greatcoat and a worn top hat. He held a rider's crop in his right hand, the reins in the other, watching the scene play out before him.

He had locked eyes with the beautiful woman just before Jasper forced her into the carriage. Although it was brief, he saw her stunning green eyes, the color of a green peepal leaf. It reminded him of the majestic broad-leaf tree he saw in the countryside of India. The woman's face was also filled with terror—the same as on the faces of men in battle before they died. That look should

29

never be on a woman's face, especially not the beautiful woman he just saw.

Damn, these men have no honor. Maybe if...No. No. No.

What was he thinking? It wasn't like him to barge into affairs that were not his own. He was here for one purpose, and one purpose only—his revenge. He had no time for a rescue mission; the girl was of no concern of his. Ali had agreed to work as Henrietta's coach driver. In return, the drug lord would locate his target. At least that was the deal he had made.

And there he was, as he promised, wearing a black velvet bowler hat, masking his features working undercover as their private carriage driver. However, Ali never thought he would find the man he sought so soon. The cad had disguised himself in western clothing so no one would recognize him, but he couldn't fool Ali Raza. He would recognize those blue eyes anywhere, and when the time was right he would take him down. He would not escape a second time.

"Driver, to the wharf, and be quick about it!" Jasper snapped in Ali's ear, disrupting his thoughts. With a quick flicker of the reins, the horses cantered down the stone alley, into the quiet, dark London streets.

As the carriage made its way through the streets, everything seemed quiet...too quiet. Not a soul was in sight, and the air was thick with tension. His target situated right underneath him, Ali remained where he sat. Ever still, until the opportunity presented itself.

The hours crawled by before the carriage had made its arrival at the wharf located on the outskirts of the city. When the vehicle came to a stop, Ali continued to stand his ground. He watched as Jasper and Oliver hauled the girl into the abandoned building. A strange feeling pricked his entire body. *This is a bad idea.* Agitated, Ali was unable to stay in the driver's seat, and thus jumped from the carriage. He paced, hands on his hips, deliberating his next move. The appearance of the woman vastly complicated his plans. Now, whatever move he made might also risk her life.

"Damn," he growled in defeat as he sprinted to another entrance into the building.

The building appeared in desperate need of repair. The windows were filthy and broken. The floorboards warped in various places, with nails stretching from their encasement. Boxes, crates, barrels, and sacks lined the walls—untouched since the day of its production. Coiled ropes lay in bundles on the dusty floor. The rods of upper-level catwalk clung to the ceiling for dear life, hanging by scraps of rusted metal. Charmaine came to the conclusion that the building hadn't operated in years, given the current condition it was in.

The floorboards echoed under Charmaine's feet as Oliver and Jasper dragged her inside, the blue-eyed man following behind. It was a wonder that she didn't trip over her own feet as Oliver shoved her into a chair. Charmaine swung one foot out to try kick Oliver in the shin, but missed.

Jonathan, the man who watched over Henrietta, remained ever stoic. A towering, robust figure from what she could tell. He folded his dark arms across his large chest, stretching the fabric of his white button-down shirt. His black bowler situated over eyes covered most of his features, except for a curved nose.

Oliver walked a full circle around Charmaine, eyeing her. It was ages before he spoke. "What were you doing in the shop? And why were you spying?"

"Spying? Nothing could be further from the truth! I work as Henrietta's assistant; I was closing the shop down for the night. I was bringing the day's earnings to her, like I always do. As I got closer to her office I heard voices, your voices from the back room; eavesdropping was an accident." Charmaine tried to appear calm, despite the thundering in her chest.

"And I suppose ye had no intention of tellin' the Bobbies, huh?" Charmaine didn't answer.

"I asked you a question," Oliver snarled. "You think yer so smart by remaining silent."

"Only compared to some," she breathed out.

"A bit of a wise ass aren't we? We'll see how smart you are when we give you a potion."

Charmaine didn't know what that meant, but she didn't like it. Oliver motioned to Jasper, calling him over. Jasper brought with him a leather box. Inside, it contained several white paper packets, all stacked on top of one another. Oliver took one of the small white triangular packets in his hand as he spoke.

"This, this right here is pure opium. Straight from the sub-continent. I think it will prove successful in the streets of merry London. It only needs testing. And take a guess who our test subject is going to be."

Charmaine blanched, and heart just jumped into her throat—her. "That's right, sweetheart," said the blond.

"If you think for one minute…"

"You don't get a choice. Hold her arms, boys," Oliver announced as Charmaine shot up from her seat, only to be forced back down by Jasper and the blue-eyed man.

Charmaine struggled with all her might to break free from the iron grip the men had on her. Swinging her right leg in the air, it made contact, right into Oliver's groin. Charmaine knew the consequences of her actions, but she didn't care.

Oliver doubled over in pain, releasing one of her arms during the struggle. Charmaine back-handed Jasper in the nose.

"Yow!" Jasper let out a yelp of pain.

With one free arm, while covering his nose, Jasper forced Charmaine back into the chair at full force, almost toppling it in the process.

"You bitch! I'll teach you a lesson you won't soon forget." Charmaine closed her eyes, and turned away as Jasper raised his hand to strike. When nothing came,

Charmaine opened one eye to see the intervention. It was the coach driver who stopped Jasper's hand from striking.

"What in the hell do you think you're doing!" Jasper yelled out.

"You touch one hair on the lady's head, you will regret it," the mysterious man threatened. Jasper opened his mouth to say something, but didn't have the chance. The newcomer twisted his hand in a circular motion. Jasper cried out, clutching the injured hand, dropping to one knee in pain.

The handsome stranger threw off his top hat and tossed his white scarf aside. He stepped forward to Jasper and lashed him across the face with the riding crop, sending the henchman to the floor, this time in excruciating pain. Jonathan, the larger man who had remained silent, now charged towards him. The mysterious man side-kicked Jonathan in the chest, catapulting him backward into Oliver, knocking both men to the ground in one fell swoop.

Charmaine couldn't believe what she was seeing. She'd never seen anyone take on three men single-handedly He had saved her life.

"Come, we must get you out of here." Without waiting for a response, he took her hand and hauled her from the chair. Charmaine gave no resistance and did as she was told. Despite his pain, Jonathan rolled to one side and reached for his holster, pulling out his pistol.

Shots rang out as Charmaine and Ali ducked the oncoming bullets. The shots Jonathan delivered missed, instead shattering crates full of freight, sending debris throughout the warehouse. Charmaine continued to run as the handsome stranger urged.

Pitink! Patink! Patink! The stray bullets continued to fire from Jonathan's gun. Groaning from the onslaught, the tension rods of the steel catwalk began to strain under the pressure and broke free from the ceiling. Wood, steel, and bolts cascaded from above, crashing together in a plume of dust, narrowing the escape from the would-be disaster. Charmaine could hear Oliver's voice in the background.

"Go after them, you fools! She knows!"

Charmaine and Ali continued to run despite the gunfire spraying around them. She began to think they might not make it out alive, until they had reached a door. The carriage remained where the henchmen had left it. Ali jumped into the driver's seat, pulling Charmaine next to him. In one fluid motion, Ali flicked the reins of horses, causing them to rear back and charge into a full gallop. At that moment the back door burst opened. Jasper, Oliver, and Jonathan continued to shoot into the darkness of night as they faded out of sight.

Chapter 5

The dawn was on the rise when the large black carriage reached the outskirts of London town. Dozing off and on, Charmaine tried to wind down from the previous night's events, but, try as she might, it was of no use. Growing frustrated, she gave up the idea of sleep and sat up in her seat. Laying her head down on the dark wooden ledge, she looked up at the mysterious carriage driver, curious as to why he'd saved her life, or what he was doing here.

He could have left me there at the wharf without a care…or dropped me on the edge of town, and had me walk back without hesitation. And how did he know about Henrietta? How are they connected?

Charmaine considered of a multitude of reasons on the hows and whys of the situation. She was so lost in thought that she didn't realize she she'd been staring at him for quite some time.

"Is something amiss?" He finally spoke up.

"Why did you save me?" Charmaine blurted out without thinking.

"Out of instinct. I could not leave a damsel in distress…is that how you say it?" A rich, smoky accent slipped through.

"You could have left me at the edge of town easily and been about your way."

Ali gave her a quizzical look at the question.

"True. Yet, a gentleman always makes sure a lady is safe before his duty is complete.

It was her turn to give a quizzical look. *Lady*? She wasn't used to that word. At least not in a long time.

"I want to thank you for last night. I was too…frazzled to mention it before."

"You were in a dangerous situation; I imagine you would be. You can call me Ali Raza."

My word.

He was a fine specimen—his rolled cotton sleeves outlined his powerful arms, flowing black locks, mahogany brown eyes, and each little muscle moving with a flicker of the reins. Small bits of hair began to form a five o'clock shadow along his chiseled jaw line; his eyes were dark, no doubt weary from last night. She saw him in the morning light of day, and a warm feeling began to resonate throughout her entire body.

"Charmaine Radcliff. Your English, it's fluent. How long have you spoken it?"

"All of my life."

"Truly?"

"Yes. I can speak many languages, but English is taught to us at an early age. If we don't learn where I'm from, no one would be able to understand each other, because of so many dialects." His voice dipped and rose as he emphasized his words.

"Where are you from?"

"India."

"India…" she repeated. "What are you doing here? You're a long way from home."

"I don't have a home. It's a long story."

"Oh. I'm sorry."

"No, think nothing of it." He gave her a slight, lopsided smile.

An awkward silence filled the space between the two. Charmaine shifted her eyes down, like a child after they have misbehaved. Her green eyes were hollow of emotion. Ali must have read her thoughts, for when Charmaine lifted her head up she saw him reach around to the satchel and pull out his wool army topcoat.

"Here, put this on; you must be freezing," she heard him say as he wrapped the jacket around her shoulders, with the reins between his knees.

"Thank you." She blushed at the sentiment. Charmaine tilted her head to one side, catching an unfamiliar smell. Sandalwood. The scent lingered on the fabric, and brought an unusual balm upon her person.

"I just thought of something," she said. "We are allies, are we not? India and Britain, I mean."

Ali flinched at that statement, remembering the incident in the Thar.

"In a way, although there are misconceptions." He thought over the choice words with care.

"Such as?"

"Agreements on the East India Company."

"But the Company ended over 30 years ago. Why would there be misconceptions?"

"Because the British superpowers want to re-establish the trade. On their terms for dominance of power, they still have a foothold in my country, and with no plans of leaving anytime soon. My superior officers do what they can to keep the peace and to prevent another war from breaking out."

"I had no idea," she whispered, feeling ashamed of the statement.

"Many people do not. And that's why many people despise other countries with so much power. They think they can wage war on a country that has little or no experience with defending themselves. Foreign invaders feel entitled to such liberties. They can't see past their own blind greed to see what is on the other side to see the truth. They are hurting other innocents who have nothing to do with the situation—others who won't comply with their law. It doesn't mean they are bad, only…" Ali trailed off.

"The superpower wants more power, to become dominate," Charmaine finished for him.

"Yes, exactly." A ghost of a smile appeared across his features. "That's why there is a lot of killing and war. It's because neither side will accept defeat."

"Are you…Do you?" She hesitated to ask.

"I am—or was, a solider, until a short time ago." He faced forward. "I've fallen from grace."

"I see." Charmaine meekly answered.

~*~*~

He caught himself staring at her yet again. Did he smile?

That was twice now. I have not smiled in years. What was happening to him?

He became sullen, going back to the memories he had of that day. When his entire life around him ceased. That day was the day he had fallen off God's map, and into purgatory.

The sound of the horses trotting on the pavement was the only sound echoing in the chilled morning air, as silence again had befallen the carriage. A short time later they arrived in front of a small abbey. Charmaine was working on descending the carriage when Ali rounded the other side to help her down. He took her hand when the hem of her dress caught on a loose piece of edging jutting from the carriage. Holding onto her waist, he lifted her down as if she weighed nothing. He held on a bit longer than was appropriate.

"Thank you." She eyed him before glancing away, her heart hammering in her chest.

"Not at all." He let her go and placed his hands in his pockets.

"An abbey? Why have we stopped here?" Charmaine cleared her throat as a way to clear the tension.

"I figured you would be safer here. Those men will be after you sooner or later. No one will think to look for you here. You should not go back to your home yet. That is the first place they will look."

That's a good idea. However, Papa will be worried sick about me.

"What about you?" she called to him as he began to walk away.

"Don't worry about me. I'm no stranger to danger."

"If it's any importance, I may be of some use to you."

"Of use? How?" he pronounced thickly as he turned toward her.

"I know this city inside and out. Whatever you are looking for, I may be able to help. Although you and I just met, in time you will be able to trust me enough to let me in on your tryst."

"Madam, I have not stayed alive this long because I let anyone in on my trysts. I've stayed alive long enough because I work alone. I've saved your life, and now I have nothing left to say or do. Good day."

She panicked. She couldn't let him just walk away; she needed to get to the police, to rid herself of Henrietta, to get home…to resolve this whole mess she was in. "Then what do you have left to lose?"

~*~*~

He stopped in his tracks. That got his attention. *I could lose my life, the remainder of my sanity, appendages. Among other things…*

"You have a lot of spirit for a woman who just met a stranger." He turned to face her.

"And you are rather cheeky for a man; more than my liking. After your daring rescue at the wharf, I figure we are no longer strangers."

"What makes you think I won't whisk you away to where no one can find you?

"Haven't you already?"

Point.

"Or seduce you when given the opportunity?" he asked, slowly striding in her direction.

"I would assume for a gentleman of your standing, you would do no such thing. "

"How would you know where I stand?" he challenged.

"The jacket you offered me in the carriage, it's of military make. I would assume as a military officer, you are—were of high standing. Plus, the mannerisms and gestures you have shown so far speak thus. Not to mention, if you were not you would have ravished me by now." That rendered him speechless. "What I require, sir, is protection. Your protection. A bodyguard if you will. Like you said before, those men could be back to finish the job.

After what I saw back there at the shop, I am not looking forward to the outcome, and staying in some abbey will not suffice fully. So, what say you, sir?"

He thought about it for a while. Staring at her.

"All right. You win for now. I may be a gentleman, but I am no saint. And don't think this is over. I'm here for one thing, and one thing only. I will not have any interference, nor are you allowed to leave the safety of this building without me present. Is that understood?"

She harrumphed. "Understood." She held out her hand. "Deal?"

Ali stared at her hand for a long moment. Hesitating at first, he slowly reached to clasp hands to seal the deal. They broke the shake as he escorted her to the door.

"Remember, do not leave the safety of these walls for any reason. You don't know who could be lurking about. I will be here tomorrow to check on you."

Ali walked down the stairs to the carriage on the street. Jumping into the driver's seat, he flicked the reins to motion the horses forward, leaving Charmaine to her own devices.

Lifting the heavy iron knocker bolted to the door, she gave it a loud *BANG, BANG, BANG!*

The door flew open and there stood a priest, just as confused as Charmaine.

"My name is Charmaine Radcliff, and I'm in a great deal of trouble."

The priest nodded, then motioned her inside.

"I'm telling you, Missus, he was a force unlike we have ever seen before. He fought like something not of this world. I've never seen such a man." Oliver was retelling the story to Henrietta Flint, who sat behind her desk.

She gave Oliver's broken hand resting in a sling once-over. "That is the most ridiculous story I have ever heard."

The men stood their ground.

"It is all true. We would not have told you otherwise," Jasper added.

"Where is the girl? Where is Charmaine?"

"The man, the carriage driver, took her. We tried to stop them, but…we lost them."

"Well then." Henrietta rose from her desk and flattened her hands on the wooden surface. "Well then, it is up to you three to find them. And when you do, you will bring the girl to me." She scanned each face. "Do I make myself crystal clear?" All three men nodded in compliance.

Chapter 6

"Have you noticed anything peculiar about her behavior before the disappearance, Mr. Radcliff?"

The Chief of Scotland Yard spoke with Charmaine's father, Arthur Radcliff, the following night.

"I don't believe so." Arthur folded his arms across his chest. He released a sigh, deep in thought.

After a few minutes of silence, he spoke. "I have not seen any changes in her behavior. Charmaine has always been a sensible girl. I just don't understand how this could have happened." Arthur brushed his fingertips along his mustache. "She always returns home when she finished working with Mrs. Flint, yet—"

"Did you say Flint?" the Chief Inspector interrupted hastily. "Henrietta Flint?"

"Why, yes, but I don't see how she has anything to do with this." Arthur looked up from his thoughts to address the chief.

"Mrs. Flint is the number one suspect in this case, since she was the last person to see your daughter before her disappearance. We have reason to believe she may have something to do with the incident." The Chief Inspector placed his pen and paper in the inner pocket of his coat. "Rest assured, Mr. Radcliff, we will do everything in our power to find your daughter. If she is in this city, we'll find her." The Chief Inspector ushered his men to the door; Arthur followed behind.

"Thank you, sir," Mr. Radcliff said as he escorted the chief out. Flashes of light illuminated the room, indicating the impending storm.

Arthur Radcliff turned to the window as he combed his through his chestnut hair. His once- handsome features were now lined by years of wear. A soft whisper escaped his lips. "Charmaine, where could have you gone?"

When morning arrived at the abbey, Ali awaited on the steps as promised. Beside him rested his leather satchel and a large white box. In his hands he held the slender, gold-encrusted dagger. Taking his index and middle fingers, he glided them across the smooth steel. His thoughts trickled back to that day in the desert.

Ali couldn't help but wonder that the blue-eyed man he saw in Kolachi resembled Suneel. *But, that doesn't make sense. Why would a solider of reputable standing commit such a crime? Why? To what purpose?*

Agitated, he gripped the hilt with his left hand to release some of the built-up tension. Rage began to build within. The scent of lavender disrupted his thoughts, and his ears perked up the sound of treading of footsteps descending the stairs behind him. He rose from his resting place and turned to face Charmaine. She was in the same plum-colored dress since yesterday, disheveled, but a vision in the morning light. The color had returned to her face.

Her auburn hair was pulled into a thick braid, and small wisps of hair escaped from their confines.

It was becoming increasingly uncomfortable that, every time he saw her, his heart beat with anticipation. The rage of injustice had hardened his heart against such frivolous emotions. He had never been like this before; even when he was in the heat of battle, he was always in control.

"Hello again," Charmaine spoke as she approached him.

"Hello." He held his gaze on her, struggling to pull himself together.

"What is that white box beside you?"

Turning his head to find the object in question, Ali finally strung together a cohesive answer. "For you." Ali picked up the box that stood by his feet, then handed it to her.

"For me?" She appeared shocked.

"The dress you are wearing, it is soiled and torn. I thought you may need something else to wear for the time being."

Glancing down, she noticed the tattered state of her dress. The color seemed to be the only thing intact. A button went missing and another hung by a thread. The hem opened at the seam.

She looked away. "I guess after all that has happened, I never noticed."

"Open it," he urged.

Charmaine obeyed, sinking onto the steps. A small smile crossed her lips as she lifted the cover of the encased contents.

Inside was a simple blue cotton dress with the square neckline, trimmed in white lace, and three-quarter-length sleeves. A blue silk ribbon completed the design. Holding the garment against her torso, she admired the vestment. Her fingers glided across the folds of the fabric. "It has been so long since I've had a proper dress."

Ali saw the sparkle in her eye as she descended the staircase coming towards him. Charmaine opened her mouth as if to say something else, but snapped it shut. He realized the change in her breathing; it became quicker. Scarlet stained her fair complexion, and she closed her eyes.

Ali waited a few moments before he said something. "Are you all right? Charmaine?"

In an instant, the young woman's eyes opened. "Excuse me. I need—" The reply was cut short as Charmaine leaped from the steps. And left a rather perplexed Ali to wonder what had happened.

~*~*~

Charmaine wasted no time. As she made a mad dash across the abbey garden, she threw open the brass handle to her makeshift room. The door scarcely closed behind her as she cursed herself several times. She could feel the heat radiate from her face as she placed her hands on her neck. A deep breath calmed her nerves and steadied her racing heart. Charmaine took a long look at the reflection staring back, and replayed the incident in her head.

Charmaine wondered what Ali would think of her in the dress. When she stood there on the steps of the abbey, an overpowering sense of joy empowered her person—although she remained stoic, and calm. Charmaine wanted to kiss him, an unyielding urge to press her lips against his. She often daydreamed what it would be like.

Wait, what was she thinking? This behavior was rather inappropriate for an accomplished lady. If her education taught her anything, a proper young lady is supposed to remain collected at all times—emotions were always concealed. *He'll think you impertinent. He'll leave for sure.*

But when the vision came to her, a quivering sensation foreign to her replaced the somber feeling that had engulfed her for so long. Her heart began to beat out of control. Charmaine couldn't let the wayfaring warrior see her in such a state.

Once her wits were gathered, Charmaine straightened her stance and began to unfasten the tattered dress, only to discard the disheveled garment on the bed. When the struggle ceased she took one final look in the mirror. *I only hope he doesn't think the worst of me.*

Exhaling, Charmaine forced herself out the door. She couldn't believe her luck when she rounded the corner. Ali was standing in the same spot where she'd left him. He seemed to be staring off into the distance.

Thank heavens. Charmaine placed a hand over her heart. She cleared her throat to gain his attention. He turned in her direction.

Was that a smirk tugging at his lips?

"Is something the matter?" she asked.

"No, why do you ask?"

"You're staring."

"My apologies." He shook his head to snap himself out of it. "Shall we get down to business then?"

Chapter 7

Ali and Charmaine searched the entire city. Questioning every weapons dealer and small arms shop they could find for clues relating to his dagger, but every clerk had the same story:. It was too unique to replicate. No one had seen it's equal.

It had been custom-made. Where did it come from? He had spent too much time on this. The trail was growing cold. Ali began to give up hope. He'd had his chance to apprehend the man in the black derby hat days ago, when he rescued Charmaine. But the opportunity slipped through his fingers. He rescued the girl out of instinct, although he didn't have to. His face came to mind; if his memory was correct, Henrietta had called him Johnathan. Everything was fragmented. The circumstance was an enigma he couldn't piece together.

He grew silent, and said little the entire time.

"Ali, this may not be the opportune moment," Charmaine said, breaking the silence, "but I was thinking of writing my father, to inform him of my safety."

"That may not be a wise idea. It might draw attention to you and your father." His slight accent slipped through.

"I know, I'm just so worried for him. I promise to be discreet. Only to tell him I am all right, and I'm safe. He must be sick with worry. Would you take it to him?"

"I do not even know where you live."

"I can write down the address for you. Are you able to navigate the city without me?"

"Can I navigate?" He scoffed. "I can navigate a platoon through a desert sandstorm," Ali replied rather presumptuously.

"So, you'll do it?"

"All right, but do not say where you are, whatever you do."

"I won't. And thank you."

A shutter wracked his body, breaking his reverie. His ears perked up at the sound of voices floating from behind, awfully familiar voices. Instinctively, Ali pulled Charmaine into the alley. He shielded her with his body so she wouldn't be seen. Ali peeked his head out from around the corner, he spotted Oliver and Jasper rounding the corner. They were walking straight in their direction.

It was only a matter of time.

"Jasper, what are we doing? We've been searching since morning for those two and we haven't had supper yet. Can't we call it a day? My feet are achin' something fierce, and blisterin'."

"Shut it, Oliver. If we let that tart get away, she'll spring the whole operation wide open. Besides, I want revenge for her kicking me in my jewels."

"If we haven't found any traces of them now, I don't think we will anytime soon. Come on."

Ali could feel Charmaine tremble next to him, and sense her heart beat begin to quicken. She began to struggle. The last think Ali needed was for her to panic and give away their presence.

He could hear Oliver and Jasper approaching, closer and closer. He could have thought of other ways to protect her, but he needed to act fast; he didn't have time to think. Easing her to the wall of the building, he wrapped his arms around her to suppress her trepidation. Without a second thought he swooped down, crushing his lips against hers—shielding her face from view.

Her lips, those supple lips, were torturing him; to his surprise they were moving with his, calling out for more. His entire body electrified. It had been too long since he'd been with a woman. He had thought what it would be like to kiss this woman. Often wondering what her velvety lips would taste like. What they'd feel like against his. The intoxicating lavender scent that filled his mind, paralyzing him from common sense and tugging at the fibers of his being. Impulse clouded his thinking. His hands slid down to her waist, pulling her even closer, enveloping her further in his embrace. He heard a soft sigh escape her. If he thought she would no longer haunt his thoughts, he was sadly mistaken.

Oh, God! My restraint is being sorely tested. Nothing good can come from this. He hadn't felt like this in a long while. The electricity they ignited turned into fire. He had to stop this before he lost complete control.

Charmaine didn't know what to think. She couldn't think. Elation, confusion, and relaxation overpowered her senses. Her shaking ceased almost immediately when he kissed her. She had never kissed like this before; indeed, she had never kissed at all!

It was empowering, magnificent!

It wasn't right. Something like this was too good to be true. It had to stop but she couldn't, and didn't want to. Without a care she moved her hands to his chest, inching toward the collar of his shirt. It seemed like the only thing holding her up was his powerful arms.

Don't stop, don't stop.

Heat was building—a magnificent feeling intensifying in her lower regions. Dizzied by the newfound passion, her judgment was clouded, her limbs weakened. Would she faint? She could hear voices trailing off. Then suddenly he pulled away. Charmaine fought to compose herself. Encompassed in her daze, she could hear his voice from far away.

"Come, they are gone."

Ali tugged her out of the alley, pulling her from the dream-like state.

Chapter 8

The moon provided enough light as Ali raced across the lawn of the Headquarters of the Royal Army that was situated in the heart of downtown. In the moonlight, the headquarters stood as a majestic two- story stone structure. Paneled windows lined the early Victorian structure to provide an ample view of the surrounding area. Ali barely made it inside the perimeter, unseen by the passing guards. He lifted the sill of lower-level window with ease, and slipped inside.

So far so good. My skills are paying off.

Now, the real test would be making his way into the personnel office with the remaining security roaming about. It was a miracle Ali was able to locate anything in maze-like building. The dark provided the perfect camouflage, so Ali was able to slip in and out of the shadows unseen. The sound of approaching footsteps alerted Ali; two guards rounded the corner. He pressed himself against the wall, and uttered a string of curses in Urdu. Maybe he should have brought Charmaine with him instead of leaving her at the abbey; she could have distracted the guards whilst Ali could slink around unseen.

When he deemed it safe, Ali emerged from the shadows to follow behind the guards who were too lost in conversation to notice him. It was a longshot to find the correct office, but they might lead him where he needed to be.

He continued to follow the guards until he came upon a line of doors. He again pressed himself into a dark space until the watchmen were out of sight to make his move. Ali crept to a row of offices, names etched on gold plaques. Ali steadied his hand on every doorknob. Locked. It didn't matter—they were not what he was searching for.

He made it to a flight of stairs, climbing to the top floor unnoticed. A faint glow of lamplight flickered at the corner of his eye. Lo and behold! It was coming from a panel of glass.

Ali continued to creep down the narrow hall to the door marked *PERSONNEL.*

Success. Reaching into a small leather case attached to his belt, he pulled out a soft brown cloth containing an assortment of slender metal lock picks. Ali inserted the pick into the keyhole, maneuvering the small tool in several positions until *Click!* The locking mechanism popped open.

He replaced the tool and slipped inside. A quick glance about the room, Ali sought clues. Any clues. He turned and noticed a desk; beside it, a tall file cabinet. Ali silently stepped to the desk. He pulled out each drawer, only to find nothing but stationery items. When he turned to pull the file drawers, some relief flooded his being. Rows and rows of records filled the space.

Nothing. Nothing. Nothing. Damn! Wait, what's this? The name Radcliff peeked out from the folder, which captured his attention.

"Tate, William."

Opening the file, he skimmed the information printed on the papers. There, in black and white typed lettering, was the Radcliff name. A statement written by the police, from Arthur and Charmaine. His eyebrows rose in alarm. *This William Tate must be on a high-alert watch.* He glanced over his shoulder as he folded one of the papers, and placed the items in his satchel.

Ali placed the file into its home, and continued to search the remaining files for his object of interest. With each stroke of his fingers he came up with nothing, until a special file marked CONFIDENTIAL caught his sight. Ali pulled the file from its resting place and began reading.

"Oh, really? That's how you're going to play the game, Jonathan Conroy? Not while I have anything to say about it."

Sounds of boots clicking against tile caught Ali's attention. Voices of the guards were coming around his way. Ali slid into the shadow of the wall of the office until the footsteps and voices passed. Folding the documents several times, he slipped them into the satchel. Ever so gently, he replaced the file jacket back in the cabinet, and pushed the drawer in before jumping out the second-story window.

"It's bloody freezing," Oliver grumbled as he placed his hands under his arms to keep warm. "How long do they expect us to stay out here, Jasper?"

"Quit yer bellyachin'. We have a job to do, remember? The boss told us to wait outside this Radcliff's place until he comes out, then follow 'im. Those were the orders."

"I don't trust 'enrietta. She seems to be too much of a harpy," Oliver sneered while breathing into his hands, then tucked them back underneath his arms.

With the missive in his shirt pocket, the sound of voices in the distance caught Ali's attentions. He stopped short to listen. *It couldn't be…*It was Jasper and Oliver, and they were near Charmaine's house. *Uh oh, not those two again.*

"Come off it; we shouldn't be for much longer." He heard the voice of Jasper and darted behind a neighbor's house. Ali waited in the dark as he watched for the two henchmen to make their move.

It probably isn't a good idea to tell Charmaine that I saw them. She'll worry more than she needs to.
The door to the Radcliff home opened. Charmaine's father, Mr. Radcliff, appeared on the other side of the threshold. He stepped onto the street, unaware of Oliver and Jasper's presence as they followed several paces behind the elder. When he assumed it was safe, Ali materialized from his haven and skimmed to the door. He shoved Charmaine's message through the crack of the entry. Then he made a mad dash to follow Mr. Radcliff, to make sure he was unharmed.

At twilight the next day, after some much-needed rest, Ali walked up to the back door of the abbey where Charmaine resided. It had been a full week and four days since he'd first met Charmaine

Radcliff and saved her from an uncertain fate. The work they had accomplished had proven successful, despite his self-doubts. Now, the only thing left was to keep her out of trouble until he could find the answers he sought, quite certain she could provide them. He wouldn't be surprised if there was another attack on Charmaine, since Jasper and Oliver were roaming in the shadows somewhere.

He found it hard to breathe, and tugged at his collar with his index finger for some invisible form of relief. A smile pulled at his lips at the thought of the passionate kiss in the alley. He hadn't kissed like that since…since he didn't know how long! Such passion and such heat. His lower extremities were tingling at the thought of his hands on her lower backside. The memory of lavender scent filled his senses. His loins tightened at the thought of his hand caressing…

Banish the thought, man; keep it together! You have a job to do. There will be no time for dalliances. This is not suitable behavior of a gentleman. He cleared his throat, cursing, trying to pull himself together. He needed to clear his mind.

He couldn't visit often; there was a risk of being seen like this that could spell disaster. Especially for Charmaine; it would not be proper for her to be alone with him any longer. Ali needed to withdraw himself from any further…distractions. Before this situation with Charmaine got out of hand, this mission had to be accomplished, and soon.

Ali continued his stride through the colorful garden, up to the oak door. He gave his collar a tug, adjusted it to a comfortable position before stepping through the portal. All was quiet. He looked around the room before calling out to her.

"Charmaine?" Someone crept forward. Before he could react, a heavy object hit him sending him into oblivion.

~*~*~

"Oh, Ali! Where did you come from?" Charmaine gasped.

She didn't know what came over her. That had always been her problem, acting before thinking.

Charmaine was at his side in less than a second. Brushing her hand across his head, she checked for any damage. No one had ever ruffled her feathers like he did. She inspected the tender, round, red lump that was beginning to form on his forehead.

Oh, why did you have to be so… so…! She couldn't finish the sentence due to her agitation.

"Uggghhh…" she groaned out, using all her strength to move his unconscious body to the bed before he woke.

She made the effort to lift him up onto the bed before losing grip. "So damn heavy."

Thud! His body fell straight to the floor.

"Sorry," she whispered.

She made another attempt to lift Ali onto the mattress. "Heave…Ho!" Her feet slipped. In an instant Charmaine skidded on the braided rug, landing on top of him.

"UMPH!"

Finally, at least half of him was on the bed. The urge to take advantage of the moment overwhelmed her; her hand moved and paused, trailing up his chest. Her hand reached the shirt pocket.

Nothing, it's empty. He did it. She looked down at him. *Such a beautiful man…*

Charmaine's eyes glimmered. She brushed a stray lock of hair from his forehead; underneath, the bump began to protrude. Her fingertips traced his coal black hair, down to his long eyelashes and to his face. She ran her fingers along his chiseled jaw bone and then over the curvature of his lips. She moved a tiny bit closer, captivated by the man in front of her. When she gained her courage, Charmaine bent down to Ali's lips. That overpowering urge to kiss him returned, since Ali kissed her passionately in the alley. Only this time, the sensation began to burn. Charmaine stopped short when sounds began to emanate from him. Half of him was still hung off the edge and she was determined to bring all of him to the resting place. First, she pulled his knee-high boots from his feet, then lifted his muscular limbs onto the mattress.

When all was settled, the seamstress retrieved a water basin to mop his head. Water droplets trickled down his temples. He tilted his head from side to side a few times before his eyes fluttered open. It took him a few seconds to focus before regaining his senses. His hand fluttered to his head, where the lump swelled and ached. He winced from the pain.

Ali tried to get up, but Charmaine placed a hand on his chest and eased him down into the pillow. He released a groan.

"Don't get up; it will make the pain worse." She left a lingering hand on his chest.

Realizing her blunder once again, she removed it without a second thought. Turning to the wash basin, she wrung out the cloth and reapplied it to the round, red, tender area.

"What happened? The last thing I remember, I called your name. The next, I wake up like this, on the bed accompanied by splitting headache."

"I'm afraid, I attacked you with the bed warmer."

"What brought upon this urge to hit me atop the head all of a sudden?"

"I thought—I thought you were an intruder. Oliver, or Jasper. And, I was frantic." She trailed off, turning her head to hide the flush beginning to form. "I'm sorry, I don't know what came over me…"

Ali reached to turn her chin, only to pull away. "I swear, woman, you will be the death of me," Ali bit out as he closed his eyes.

Chapter 9

Charmaine closed a book and put it back in the open space on the bookshelf.

"Nothing."

Their second course of action: Search whatever they could find at the Public Library of London, located on St. James Square. Since the wild goose chase around the city proved fruitless, the only other option to retrieve any information would be through the history books. They had decided to take up a table at the farthest-most corner of the library. They wanted to hide from any possible disturbance.

Charmaine went through one book after another. She was about to give up hope of ever finding anything. Taking a break, she sauntered back to the table where Ali made himself comfortable. Hands on her hips, in the most unladylike manner, she stood there and slowly released a sigh. One hand went to the back of her neck to release the tension there.

Ali saw the gesture. He couldn't help himself. He imagined himself the one relieving the pain.

"What exactly are we looking for?" Her voice snapped him out of his daydream.

"Anything relating to this." Turning around, he retrieved the weapon from inside satchel hanging off the chair. A moment later she walked back to his side, still holding the weighty piece in her hands.

"It looks pretty new; I don't believe it would be in any of the history books. I believe I looked in every history book on the shelves."

It's the most reputable library in the country. It may not be the exact copy, but he was hoping they could find something similar. He showed the jeweled knife to Charmaine before they came to the library, hoping to jog her memory.

"I wasn't able to find anything in any of the weaponry books. What if we look during the time India was...explored?" She chose her words with care. "Do you think it would show up as something similar?"

"It is worth a try."

Hope swelled in his chest.

Charmaine strolled back to the history section, her dress swaying. She was teasing him in the most painful way. And she used it to her advantage. In the meantime, he decided to bide his time. He swung his feet on top of the table, tipping his chair back, and balanced on the back two legs. Closing his eyes, he began to daydream of soft lips.

"How convenient is this?" he heard her voice calling a while later.

"Pardon?" His eyes were still closed.

"I think I may have found something."

She materialized out of nowhere. "Auughh." A short sound escaped him when Charmaine pushed his feet off from their resting place, eyes wide, catching him off guard. Alert, he was able to react in time before meeting the table face -first.

"*The Decisive Battles of India: from 1746-1849*, by G.B. Malleson." She placed the book on the table where his feet once rested, and began flipping through the pages.

"Could this be what you are looking for?" She moved back to her seat.

And there it was. The page held what appeared to be a photo of a replica of his dagger, on the sash of an Indian Army officer. And next to the photo was a side box explaining the weaponry used in the battles.

"The Kindjal Dagger…"

Ali leaned in closer so he could read the small text, making it harder for her to concentrate on what she was reading.

"What does it say?" he asked.

"Circa 1820-50. Evolved around the region of Turkey, migrated to Russia…made of steel and wood. Ranges in (58.2 cm) 23 inches long.

"…The slender blade. Classified as a short sword …makes a good weapon for kissing." His concentration was losing the battle to her scent.

"For what?"

"For killing, easy maneuvering in short distances. Killing the enemy…" He could hear her breath quicken. Her fair complexion was flushed. She moved the book in his direction to see the photo of the weapon. "Here, does this look similar?"

Resting a hand on the back of her neck, Charmaine closed her eyes and released a smooth sigh—alleviating some of the embarrassment.

He continued to read to himself. "The dagger, being slender in size, is made up of a dark wood for the hilt with a small flower or star-like shape at the top, reaching down to the blade made of a steel-like metal. Decorated with gold flowers, typical of the Turkish/Arabic tradition…"

So, it came from that region. Of course. How else could have it traveled all the way to India? It was custom-made. It is almost identical; he had to have paid a hefty price for it. The old man was right.

When Ali came out from his thought he noticed Charmaine with her eyes closed, concentrating on her breathing. She seemed nervous around him. She didn't act like this the other day. A devilish smirk played upon his lips.

"Would you like to know what else the Indians are known for?" He spoke huskily.

Charmaine opened her eyes and started to answer him. But Ali continued to talk.

Ali continued. "They are also known for their lovemaking skills. They invented the Kama Sutra. The Caliph would have as many as seven wives, practicing with each.

"He sounds like a scoundrel…" she whispered, and rose from the chair, sliding it in between the two of them so Ali could not get any closer.

"The women would compete amongst each another for a chance to be number one. The women loved it…as did the Caliphs."

He continued, unimpeded by the chair's position. He came towards her as she backed away. Heat colored her features, her heart thundering in her chest.

"The women don't sound any better."

"Perhaps. But only the rarest of beauties would win a seat. Or the heart of the highest powers in history. And the secret was…They loved it."

"I don't think…think this is something…I should be hearing…" She panted her words out in small gasps.

Placing on hand on the wall to brace himself, he leaned in to whisper into her ear…

"I could teach you…"

She was rendered powerless. Pinned against the wall by his hard body, she stifled her breath as he traced her jawline with the knuckle of his index finger.

He inched closer. Closing his eyes, a feather-like caress nuzzled the crease of her ear with the bristle of his chin.

Trailing down her neck, moving to her shoulder, he placed slow torturous kisses that she had no control over. He had her in his grasp. Each kiss sent pulsating tremors throughout her body. Her breathing was rapid when he moved to catch her lips. His lips moved with hers in a passionate and heated kiss. She relented to him.

Moving his hands up and down, caressing her soft backside, he let out a groan, wanting more. He, in his crazed-state, moved his hands to squeeze. More and more, he became aroused with each touch. His muscular hands were beginning to stray upward, discovering the lace drawers guarding her naked thighs underneath. His feverish response was instant. He could feel her grasping the folds of his collar as he caressed the silken flesh. "You don't know how much I want you right now…I'm going mad." His voice was ragged against her lips. His arousal was cradled between her legs.

Ali didn't need any confirmation; hearing her soft sigh from the pleasure was his answer.

Suddenly, a powerful surge of emotions, feelings, and temptation flooded his being. His arousal began to throb, and he felt as if he were on fire.

The scent of sandalwood paralyzed her senses. He pressed her against the wall with his muscular frame. A dizzying sensation clouded her senses as he traced her jaw with his fingers. Bringing his face close to hers, she felt a haze surround her as he nuzzled her ear with soft kisses.

She grasped the collar of his shirt to keep from falling. His fingers found the flesh covered by dark curls in her lower region. A thrill shot through her body; her legs were to nearly ready to collapse as if they were candle wax.

Heat flooded her body, pooling in her lower region. She removed her hands to wrap her fingers in his soft raven hair as he captured her mouth, teasing her tongue. He moved his hands to the soft skin of her backside, making their way around the material of her drawers to caress the naked flesh underneath. She couldn't breathe. All she could do was feel.

And it felt so…heady, so sensual. William had never made such advances towards her. Now that she had felt this she didn't want it to end. It was too good to be real.

Wait a moment… this needs to stop. The cloud of euphoria dissipated. She was acting wantonly. What if someone discovered them like this? Low murmurs of voices echoing through the building brought her back to reality. No. No matter how much she didn't want to stop, she had to stop this insanity. "You mustn't…do that," she managed to whisper.

He let go, only to cup her flushed face. Flushed from their activity. His touch thrummed throughout her entire body.

"I need you."

Her chest tightened. With her eyes closed, she tried to speak.

"What if someone should see us?" Her voice sounded hoarse, almost gone.

Ali let out a heavy sigh. Still breathless, he fixed Charmaine's dress to where it was appropriate again. He leaned into her and dropped his head on the top of hers. When he finally regained his senses, Ali cursed himself. *Damn! What have I done? I*

71

should have pulled away! He knew better than to get involved. He had crossed a dangerous line this time. He had almost ruined her. And in a public library no less. What was he thinking? He was supposed to be a gentleman. This wasn't supposed to happen. He was only supposed to keep her out of harm's way. Not seduce her. He had disgraced her. Charmaine—the very thought of her made his heart pound and his head spin.

He breathed slowly, in and out. Being around her was inevitable. He lost control every time he was near her. A tidal wave of mixed emotions he hadn't felt in ages. He had been acting upon his lust. He had lost his focus. In addition, he still had not figured out a plan that could prove his innocence.

It's all my fault. Ahmeq!

He thought about what had been taking place, and knew it had to stop. He needed to create distance, but couldn't do that until he solved his case. But while he was here, Ali could not afford anymore distractions.

Soon, he would leave England. For good. And he would no longer have his restraints tested, nor his heart broken. He would submit to his mother's wishes and marry someone his mother chose for him. No training in the world had prepared him for what he was about to do.

His heart ached for a woman he could not have and didn't deserve. It would have been easier if he were on the battlefield. Alas, he was not. So, he went with his gut instinct.

"No more distractions." He spoke his thoughts aloud to his chestnut gelding. The horse only turned to him to butt him in the head. It caught him off balance.

~*~*~

He had "acquired" the horses from Henrietta for the time being, trading one horse to the stable master for the cost of lower rent in his facility.

Ali waited outside the stone building. He noticed the weather. It had turned overcast and gray. *What an appropriate setting for a melancholy day*, he thought. Immersed in his thoughts, Ali tried to assuage the guilt he had brought upon himself. *Seducing Charmaine was a mistake*. Inhaling a deep breath, he realized that there could be no delaying it any longer.

What in the world had happened? He came here looking for a knife. Now he had a woman in his life. How had that happened? He thought back and smiled. He never expected to meet Charmaine. And he never expected to have a conversation like the one he knew he must have. Everything was such a mess; agony coursed through him. He cleared his throat to speak, struggling to find the words to say to her.

"Charmaine, I think it's time we discuss the events that have transpired. You may have realized things have gotten…out of hand. These past few days, have been…" *Incredible*. "Irresponsible. We have an agreement that I watch over you. And I believe I have overstepped my boundaries with you. And I want to apologize for any disrespect that I may have caused you. As I have said before, I have a mission to complete, I—I cannot allow anymore distractions. I will remain your bodyguard. But, we must remain strict professionals. Do you understand?"

73

He glanced in her direction to find her reply. When he saw her, the muted expression was his answer. She was hurting, although he could tell she was trying not to show it. He hadn't known her for long, but she was putting on a brave face. Any other woman would be hysterical. Her expression knifed him in the heart. He wanted her to say something. Yell at him, curse his name. But he wanted more than anything to hold her, to kiss her hurt away. Anything, but there was nothing but empty silence. That hurt worse than any bullet wound.

Eventually, he needed be truthful with her, even if he couldn't give her the entire truth. But he could not just continue to lie to her. He had to push her away. He would risk her life if he didn't push her away, and he swore to himself that he would not risk putting her in danger. He also knew his duty by his family, and he would not string her along any farther. That wouldn't be fair to her.

He also knew what vengeance was about and knew that, without a doubt, Henrietta would track her down. She would go to the ends of the earth and back again to find her, if necessary. People who are vengeful will stop at nothing to carry out their revenge. He was not going to stop until he solved the mystery of who sabotaged his career, and why. Was that revenge? So, he thought he understood this need.

Charmaine remained silent throughout the conversation. She sensed something like this would happen. Everything seemed too good to be true. Still, she didn't want it to believe it. She thought she was not meant to love another. The memories of William rose like bile in her throat. It was happening all over again. Only this time she had become shameless, wanton.

It took everything she had to keep herself together. She wanted to scream, cry, and throw things. But what she wanted most she realized she would not get. She wanted him to love her.

"Charmaine, did you hear me?" Ali tried to coax her to answer.

She turned away from him, and struggled to control the tears that threated to fall once again. She couldn't bear to look at him. That was her answer.

Damn, why did I have to be such a fool?

The large four-seater carriage arrived at the abbey. After a lingering silence between the two of them, she had nothing more to say to him anyway.

She rose cautiously, lifting the hem of her dress as a precaution. She looked around, checking for anything that may catch her dress as she stepped down from the carriage.

"I have something to give you." A moment later, Ali was the one to break the long, awkward silence.

He reached into the satchel to pull out a Luger semi-automatic pistol. She turned to face him, confusion crossing her features as he held the polished metal in his hand.

"Keep it safe. You're going to learn how to use that thing properly. I will be nearby to secure your safety. As soon as this mission is over, I will send word to your father. And you will be able to go home and protect yourself."

She remained silent. Her nod was the only confirmation. She turned away and walked back to the abbey.-Had he no heart? All he was thinking about was work when he was killing her from the inside out. He might as well plunge a dagger through her heart, the way he was chiseling away pieces of hers.

~*~*~

She strolled around the small gardens of the abbey, not in any hurry to return to her room. Ali said she would be able to go home. But, who knew when that would be? She yearned to be home with her father. She wanted to have her books, and her things. She wanted things to go back to the way they were.

Perhaps the splendor of the garden will calm my nerves. Chin up, she took in the beauty of roses, freesia, and the carnations, mingled together to create a soothing scent that softened any mood. Their scent created a perfume that seemed to strengthen her and calm her. She lingered and examined the various tufts of green sprouting from the foliage. It seemed to soothe her frayed nerves.

When she returned to her room in the abbey, Charmaine clutched the semi-automatic handgun Ali had given her. Closing the door she paused, looking at the weapon. She thought about the conversation. Her hand glided over the polished metal. The tears she had held back this entire time broke free; she was no longer able to control her sobbing.

She sobbed till she had nothing left inside her to cry out. Ali destroyed any chances of a stable future.

Damn him. Damn him to hell. She hated him. Despised him. She was broken and empty once again.

She should have guarded her heart. She should have put a stop to this at the beginning. It was all her fault. She had grown so accustomed to his presence. She loved his sweet kisses and took to his caresses as if she were a common street walker. And she paid the ultimate price—her heart

Chapter 10

When Ali arrived the following morning, he noticed a drastic change in her. Besides being stoic since yesterday, her eyes were swollen and red. This wasn't the woman he met weeks ago. This woman before him was unrecognizable, and he was not sure how to approach her. He wasn't sure if he should. As she climbed into the carriage next to him, she remained silent.

Ali opened his mouth to say something, but snapped it closed. He'd only make it worse. There were no words he could say to undo the mistakes he'd made.

They arrived at the training field by noon; an open farmland surrounded by oaks, birch, and pine. It provided ample room to shoot. Yet, there was enough space so it would not overwhelm.

Four dummies sat in a line at the opposite end of the field. Judging by the state of their appearance, he'd created them in haste.

Stray pieces poked from the confines of the sacks. Flour bags for heads were struggling to remain propped on broomsticks. The eyes were drawn on, looking as if a school child helped him.

Her hands once again moved to her hips, observing the terrain. One eyebrow rose with concern. *He certainly went through a lot of trouble for this. I could shoot him now and no one would know.* Charmaine took a quick survey of her surroundings. She made sure no one else could stumble upon their rendezvous.

She could hear him approaching her from behind, walking back from the carriage to retrieve the gun from his satchel. His voice echoed in the empty air as he spoke.

"The first thing you need to know about shooting a gun is how to hold it. This is a dangerous piece of equipment; it isn't a toy. One false move and the gun can go off without warning. It can kill you or the person in front of you. It is crucial that you know what to do. Now, watch what I do." Positioning his stance, feet apart, he widened his arms, placing one hand on the trigger. The other hand wrapped around the grip, pulling the safety joint back. His hand rested on the trigger. He steadied his hands on the Luger.

"When you have learned that, then you can shoot the weapon." He continued his demonstration. All of a sudden, his face went blank of expression. Bringing the pistol to eye level, he released a quiet breath as he squeezed the trigger.

A loud popping noise reverberated in her ears, indicating that the bullet found its target in the chest of the middle dummy at the far end of the field. "Your turn." Lowering the gun, he handed it off to her. *Could he be any more patronizing about it?*

"Keeps your elbows out from you. One hand under the butt of the handle. Index finger through the hole of the trigger. Keep your hands steady, take a deep breath, and pull the trigger." Agitated, she followed his instructions. Shooting for the first time in her life was a little nerve-wracking.

Ali could sense her uneasiness. To remedy the situation, he approached her from behind to steady her.

"Here, let me show you. He came to her, wrapping his muscular frame around her. His sinewy arms overlapped hers, positioning her hands to steady the gun. Her agitation rose to apprehension.

"Don't forget about the safety," he reminded her.

Strictly professional, my arse.

The sandalwood scent was faint, still clinging to his white button-down shirt. He leaned in closer. Turning her head to meet his gaze, he was a hair's breath away from her ear. Insanity had to be the intent. For a fleeting moment, she wanted to forgive him; she could see the pain in his mahogany eyes when he looked at her. It felt like an eternity had passed by the time he let go.

"Shoot," he whispered softly in her ear.

Her heart skipped a beat as he released his hold on her. Just in time for her to come back to her senses. The delirium escaped her, turning to resentment once again.

BANG! A single shot rang out from the gun, hitting its target right in the chest at the far end of the field.

"Beginner's luck; nice try, though." He uttered, trying to hide his surprise.

I'll show him beginner's luck. Charmaine positioned herself, holding the gun as instructed, then pulled the trigger.

ONE.

TWO.

THREE…!

Shots rang out from the gun, all striking the middle dummy in the lower regions.

"How is that for beginner's luck?" Tossing the empty, smoking gun to the befuddled instructor, she walked away with pride.

The dumbfounded expression on his face was confirmation that she had passed the first test.

The afternoon had grown late. Twilight was on the rise when they finished their lessons. Charmaine had learned everything Ali could teach her in one day, including five different ways to shoot a gun. She was eager to learn more, but she was still cross. She did not want to press the issue any further. She continued to remain professional, as requested from her bodyguard. She went as far as refusing any help offered.

Although she couldn't deny it, a cataclysm of emotions surged through her when she was near him. She wanted to hate him. How could it be that one small glance rendered her powerless? Still frazzled by all that had transpired she neglected any caution when stepping into the carriage, catching the hem of her dress on the same broken piece of edging. This time the flimsy fabric tore all the way to the waistline, exposing her lace stockings and thighs.

"Oh dear!" Charmaine gasped.

Ali averted his gaze. He pretended not to notice the fiasco that just took place.

"I should remember to fix that." he muttered to himself.

Horrified, Charmaine could hardly contain her dismay. Nothing like this had ever happened before. She scurried to fold the fabric to cover herself up.

Ali pretended to remain oblivious. He was doing his best to contain his expanding arousal caused by the exposed, luscious, porcelain skin. Composing himself, he straightened himself before the situation got out of control. Then it came to him.

"Here, take my top coat," he said, handing the article to her.

Charmaine accepted the offer; what other choice did she have? She had just exposed one of the most intimate parts of her body to a man she loathed. Still reeling, Charmaine struggled to contain her chagrin by hiding her face in her hands.

"Don't feel embarrassed by what happened. It was an accident that could have happened to anyone." He looked, and was somewhat amused by the occurrence. There was a slight tingle in his loins.

Charmaine looked up, brushing away a stray hair that left the knot on her head, and smiled a little. She was relieved that a lecture did not come.

"All right, maybe not anyone, but, now we have a reason to find something else for you to wear."

"I can't ask any more of you. You've already been too kind." The words fell out of her mouth before she could stop them. She was finally breaking her silent treatment towards him.

"Is it not my job to see you taken care of till my duties end? We can't have you walking about in a torn dress. You are not beggar." He gave her that lopsided grin. *He was up to something. Perhaps wanting to gain favor or redemption for his action.*

"I am a seamstress, you know I can mend the dress myself."

"Yes, but it will take time to fix. This will take not that much time, plus you can't just wear one dress all the time."

He did have a point; she couldn't wear one dress the entire time. It may be too risky to go back to the house to retrieve the remainder of her dresses. Charmaine nodded, relenting to the request.

~*~*~

They stopped at the first shop they saw as soon as they arrived into town. Charmaine suppressed a cringe. Memories of what happened weeks earlier came flooding back to her.

A wave of dizziness passed through her, and she hesitated to come down from the carriage.

"Trust me," he urged, holding out his hand.

She didn't know why she did. Something inside her told her to trust him. Closing her eyes, she swallowed an invisible breath. Ali took her hand to keep her from fainting from the carriage.

Assisting her down at a suitable speed, he motioned her to the pavement. Standing behind her, he held her shoulders. He whispered into her ear.

"I'm right behind you. You can do this." His whisper was warm on her neck. Charmaine held her breath, eyes still closed, nodded, and went inside the shop.

Charmaine was unaware that two others were right behind them as well, at a nearby café, enjoying a cigarette. Oliver spied the couple disappearing into the shop.

"Hey now, lookie what we got here, Jasper ol' boy," he mused.
Jasper cocked his head in Oliver's direction. Realizing what he was talking about, a vicious curl crossed his lips.

"Now what did I tell you, Jasper? Good things come to those who wait…" He tapped the ash onto the ground.

Chapter 11

Every dress Charmaine tried on was too bright, too tight, or too revealing. He was beginning to wonder if she was doing this on purpose. A tortuous revenge began to take shape for seducing her in the alley, then the Library. It wasn't fair of him to ask for professionalism from her after her acts.

Any other woman would have been irate. Not Charmaine. She handled herself—adequately. He admired her spirit for continuing this arrangement. He admired her courage to challenge him most of all. He could not help himself when he was around her. He had never lost control around other women; it had always been the opposite. Women usually swooned for him.

No, she was unlike any woman he had encountered. Charmaine set off a fire within him whenever she was around. Thoughts of her plagued his mind far too often. *Ouf Kudda*--Good Lord, he was becoming a besotted fool. He'll need to exercise restraint in the future, who knows what she'll do. She had already proven deadly with a gun. This pining for a tigress was out of control. He needed to learn to separate business from pleasure. It was time to concentrate on the mission. Distraction Free; for now. If only he would be able to pinpoint where he went. He may have to recruit more people for his cause. Most likely it would need to be the illiterate and destitute. Things will more than likely end in chaos if not caught in time.

Sitting in the plush, white satin chair outside the ladies' dressing room. Leaning forward, elbows on knees, he continued deep in thought. *Just where could the jackal be? And why London of all places? He would stick out of the crowd way too easy. He could have gone to Abu Dabi, or Delhi just as easy or a remote region in the Mountains. But, he more than likely he had enemies in Delhi. Or he was a go-between for those more powerful. He is more than compensated for this horrendous act. Spreading decimation wherever he goes. And could Moshin be behind it all? For what? What would he gain from all his?*

"I don't understand it." Ali murmured aloud to himself.

"I beg your pardon?" Charmaine's voice interrupted his musings.

Ali looked up from his thoughts. His vision was obscured by an expanse of fair, round breasts. Charmaine had exited the dressing room displaying the dress. Indeed, it was the lowest cut, scandalous dress she had tried on yet. And it was the most tantalizing, too. The fabric molded to her figure. Deep burgundy color highlighted her porcelain colored skin. The silk neckline draped over bosoms that overflowed their entrapment.

Red-faced and bewildered, Ali was about to open his mouth in protest. Then quickly shut it, when he realized

Charmaine was already gone. Spouting a string of curse words -- what he determined to be French--behind her.

Ali, straightening in the plush, white chair, most sheepish. His arousal triggered.

"Uff! Khuda Ki Panah…*For the sake of God*. That woman was maddening." Rolling his eyes to the ceiling.

When he caught his breath, he took a quick glanced around the small room. Making certain no one saw that scene that occurred.

This is the one. A smug smile of satisfaction crossed her lips when Charmaine re-entered the changing room.

Changing from the burgundy gown into a turquoise lace, slender cut gown put a subtle smile on her face. It was identical to the one that she had torn earlier. She asked one of the ladies to stand by to help her button the dress. A few minutes elapsed before Charmaine emerged from the dressing room. Along with a few other gowns draped over her arm. She espied him by the entrance of the shop, quite agitated. He had hands on his hips and appeared more than ready to leave.

Good…

Charmaine did not take his eyes off of him as she placed the gowns on the counter. Before finalizing the total, Ali reached over and plucked a lace shawl from one of the displays.

"This too" Ali gave a curt nod to the woman behind the counter.

Charmaine had no words for him; she only stared at him nonplused. If looks could kill, that would be the winning blow. The clerk didn't seem to notice, as she folded the gowns into parcels.

Charmaine thanked the woman behind the counter and paid for her purchases. Ali continued to standby with a growing agitation as he awaited their departure.

Upon entering the carriage, Ali spoke. "Do you not think, it would be a good idea to eat something before I return you to the abbey? I cannot help but wonder—"

"You have already done more than enough. Thank you for the offer, I have provisions at the Abbey I can eat there." One would usually face the person talking. She, remained stoic as she spoke.

She continued for him. "Jasper and Oliver could be lurking about around here, as you have suggested. It would not be wise to linger any more than we should." *She was right though. Who knows what danger he could be putting her in right now?* Releasing a sigh, he flicked the reins to motion the horses.

Chapter 12

The Stag and Rose was the noisiest establishment Ali had never been to. This was his first venture into an English pub. Judging from the scene before him, they were boisterous, rough, and littered with unsavory fellows. It seemed the occupants, men who were enjoying their ale a bit too much, were just waiting for a fight to erupt. Drinking alcoholic beverages was taboo back in India. His circle believed anything altered from its original form was a sin, and that included grapes and grain. Not that Ali cared at this point. He had committed so many sins throughout his life, what was one more to add to the list?

Yet, he had found himself at the Stag and Rose, of all places. Sulking in a dark corner of the tavern, he nursed his second pint of ale. He was already starting to feel the effects of the toxic brew. Disoriented, he was hardly able to form a coherent sentence, even when the busty tavern woman came to his table to bring him another pint. "You look a little troubled, love; want to tell Myra what has brought you down?"

Ali looked up at the woman with glassy eyes and a crooked smile.

"Women. They have caused me so many troubles, I cannot even begin to tell you them all."

She smiled. "That's why most men come to these here hovels. To drink away their problems until they have nothing left to feel. Not really any point if you ask me."

Already foxed, Ali tuned her out and rambled on.

"She's…she's nothing but a loose cannon…stubborn. She's a temptress, luring me in with her siren song. And so damned beautiful. She's such a…A woman!" He slammed his hand down on the table with such force, he almost spilled his ale.

"Women these days! Who does she think she is? I saved her life, taught her how to use a gun, and took her shopping. Then, she has the gall to drive me to the brink of insanity. Not to mention I almost made sweet, passionate love to her in a dark library, and how does she repay me? She almost shoots me in the crotch! Who does she think she is?

Myra lifted an eyebrow at that statement. "From what I hear, she sounds like a spitfire.

"But that's beside the point! The point is…"

"The point is that you fancy her, love," Myra pointed out.

"Psshhh! Don't be ridiculous woman! A man such as myself isn't bred for tomfoolery." He flailed his arms every which way. "It is an honor to die gloriously in the heat of battle. To…to obey orders when given—" Ali rambled on. "And another thing! Who does that son of a dog think he is? Did he honestly think he could just…Kill me? Over what? Jealousy? Well…I sure showed him. That *bhan chote* will regret his actions. How dare he escape me? That coward."

"My mistake, just pointing out the obvious. If your lady love has the ability to reel in a handsome young buck such as yourself, she must be well worth it," Myra opined, rendering Ali speechless. He exhaled slowly. "I have a job to do, I don't have time for dalliances with a lady love who has the power to…" Ali stopped short. He turned to the tavern woman, who could only give him a look of confirmation. "Yet, I've already have done my duty, twice now by protecting her. And how have I repaid her? I've shamed her. She doesn't deserve me." He sank down in the chair.

Myra smirked. "Yer in a bad way, captain. If I were ya, I'd go to her. Tell 'er how ya feel."

"I can't; she hates me right now." Ali sank back into his chair.

"Whatever ya did, I'm sure she'll forgive ya in time. Most women who rile themselves up for a man forgive eventually."

"You're right, you're right!" Pushing himself back, raising his left hand in the air, he wobbled as he stood. "I will tell her, get down on my knees—"

"Maybe no need to go that far…"

"But my hands are stained with blood. And my family would forbid it. She is a woman my mother has not chosen. I can't be with her, it just isn't done. It would be impossible."

"MYRA! MORE ALE!" a voice rang out from the crowd.

Myra turned her head to the voice before answering. "Pardon' for say 'in' such, sir. I'm not sure how most things work. But, I would suggest from a lady's point of view. Quit pussy foot 'in' around and tell her before she gets away. Ya only live once. And to Hell with the rules!"

She sashayed off to serve the other rowdy customers, leaving Ali in stoic silence. *Could it be possible? Have I fallen in love with Charmaine Radcliff? Come to think of it, she does stir feelings that have been dormant. Not to mention she is an excellent shot. Nothing like the women back home. An enigma.* Maybe Myra was right. All that mattered now is that she accepted him as he was, and if she did not, then he would make her see.

Rising from the chair he spoke aloud. "To Hell with the rules. I'll ask for her forgiveness!"

A familiar voice came from behind him. "You'll be asking for more than that, chum." He knew exactly who it was.

"Well, well…it's my good friends, Oliver and Jasper. How's the hand?"

"We'll be dandy once we've done away with you and that bitch whore of yours." He pulled the black bowler cap away from his eyes. "You two have caused us a lot of trouble, ya know," remarked Oliver. Pointing a finger at the thugs, Ali staggered, inebriated. "Hey! Language. You will not call her that; she's the woman I love." *Did he just say that out loud?*

"Then she can join ya after we're done with ya'. I've been wondering how sweet it is between…"

"If you ever go near her, I will tear you apart where you stand." Ali whipped his guns out from his holsters. He may be foxed, but he still knew how to handle his weapons. "And I will not finish until I take down your peddler boss and her associate. I'll take all four of you down if need be."

"Let's teach this bloke a lesson." Jasper cracked his knuckles as he accepted the challenge.

"Don't make me have you regret your actions. I don't want this to turn ugly, nor do you want me to lose patience." Ali pointed the Luger at Jasper.

"It's already turned ugly, mate, and see here, we have our orders from the Missus. We need to silence ya," Jasper explained.

Placing the gun back into its holster, Ali pushed up his sleeves further up his arms. "I see. Then I have no choice but to remove the obstacles in my path."

"Challenge accepted."

With that Ali darted forward. Oliver didn't know what hit him as he spun and fell to the hardwood floor. Ali then turned around to Jasper, elbowing him in the back of the head and sending him down to the floor with a thud.

Soon enough the entire tavern joined the brawl. Chairs, mugs, plates, and other debris began flying. Oliver smoothed his jaw where the right hook had made contact. He pulled himself up to continue the fight. He sent an uppercut punch into Ali's stomach. Soon a tango of supremacy ensued between Oliver and Ali. Neither man would let the other have the upper hand.

"I won't tell ya again, mate, I will silence you, one way or another. The wench has unfinished business with the Missus and us. I admire your fighting skills but I can't let ya go." Oliver was panting rather heavily.

"And I'll tell you as well, as a man of honor I can't allow you to do that. I have a job to finish and if I have to, I'll take her with me to the ends of the earth. If only to keep her safe from the likes of you and your boss."

Oliver lunged forward this time. Ali caught him by the elbow, blocking the impact from the blow. Although still feeling the effects of the ale, he still had a great sense of control in his movements. Punches flew left and right, until Ali finished Oliver off with a roundhouse kick that sent him flying into the wall of the tavern.

"I did not want to do this, *Yaar Panga Matley*—nor do you want to mess with me. But you two left me no other choice." His voice sounded dangerous as he spoke to the half-conscious man.

Oliver was not about to give up so easily. He kicked Ali's feet out from under him, forcing him to the floor. Ali was still struggling to compose himself when Oliver surprised him by placing Ali in a stranglehold.

Ali tried to repeal the attack, but was beginning to lose consciousness. His entire body was becoming lighter and lighter. *No! You can't let this happen, do not let him win! You need to protect Charmaine; these men will kill her. Protect her!* The beast within snapped. Ali slammed the heel of his boot into Oliver's foot.

With a yelp, Oliver loosened the sleeper-hold he had on Ali. It was his chance. Elbowing Oliver in the Adam's apple Ali slammed a final blow to his face, sending Oliver to the filthy tavern floor once again.

Rubbing the pain from his neck, he spoke to an unconscious Oliver and Jasper sprawled out on the ground. "You're lucky I didn't have to kill you; it could have been much worse." With a breath of relief, Ali put his hands on his hips, proudly puffing out his chest in victory. However, a stray empty mug hit him in the back of the head, rendering him unconscious.

Chapter 13

When Ali awoke the next morning, a splitting migraine was the only thing there to greet him. He rose from the stone slab bed bolted to the wall. Ali's head pounded and his throat felt as dry as the desert. While his stomach retaliated against movement, threatening to retch at any moment, an ache in his jaw caused him to touch his cheek. Ali hissed as twinge of pain sparked where the red bruise lay. *Why men enjoy this fowl drink is beyond me.*

The events from last night at the Stag and Rose spun through his mind. Jasper and Oliver, the fight…Ali looked around.

Where am I? Then it dawned on him. He knew where.

Charmaine, Oh God, where is Charmaine? I need to get out of here.

"Jail-keep! Jail-keep!" Despite the roiling in his gut, he scrambled to his feet and poked his head through the bars of his cell. "Jail-keep, I need to send a missive to someone, let them know—"

The guard walked to the cell and slid his Billy club over the bars to quiet Ali down. "You'll do nothing of the sort." Ali took his hands off the bars and backed away. "It's scum like you, that's what's wrong with our society."

Frustrated, he raked his hands over his head. There was no telling what sort of danger Charmaine might be in. "Damn," he cursed, pacing the jail cell. He had to find a way out of this mess. A full day had gone by, and Charmaine was growing restless because she still hadn't heard from Ali. He had told her to trust him, but she was finding it hard to do when he did not stay in contact, and when he did, he never revealed much about himself. Something didn't feel right.

All sorts of questions were spinning in her head, and most were about Ali and what kind of man he might really be. Staying hidden away at abbey was beginning to drive her mad. Her nerves were shot. She slipped through the garden gate for her daily stroll. Enjoyable as it was, the garden was doing little to calm Charmaine's turbulent thoughts, and hope was dwindling that she'd see her Papa again.

Perhaps Ali's secretive behavior was why she found it hard to trust him. He did seem sincere when he said he would protect her. It was nice to feel safe. She'd be heartsick if he left. But never to see him again? Even if he did stir her anger, she had grown so accustomed to him and to his sandalwood scent and his ability to make her weak in the knees. Charmaine wrapped her arms around her body. She shivered, missing Ali's strong, protective arms around her. The sensation thrummed throughout every fiber of her being.

His handsome face flashed in her mind; remembering the day in the field, as those strong arms encircled her being and the way he held his hands in hers.

Closing her eyes, Charmaine came to the realization that she missed him. Yes, she missed Ali, and grew worried about him. Exhaling the invisible breath she held in, Charmaine opened her eyes to look up at the sun peeking through the clouds.

Growing even more restless, Charmaine felt as if she were about to go mad. Anything to stave off her boredom. Perhaps a trip into town would stave off her anxiety.

I know Ali said not to leave the abbey grounds, but to hell with that.

Having little care, she made her way to the stables to saddle a mare for a short ride. The abbey would once in a while adopt aged horses, the animals too old to pull a carriage or preform menial labor for the city. So, they came here, to the abbey, to live out the rest of their days in peace.

The tension was more than evident. The honey - colored horse could sense her trepidation. The rapid twitching of the mare's tail almost hit Charmaine in the eye. Charmaine closed her eyes to the action. "It seems you are in need of some fresh air as well, are you?" she spoke to the mare while smoothing her coat.

~*~*~

The streets were bustling. Charmaine made her way through the throngs of people. She had located a stable near a small district of restaurants and shops. Dismounting, she gave the reins to the stable master. She handed him a guinea for his trouble; the man nodded in response to the coin.

Turning to leave, a flash of color caught her eye from across the road. A gaggle of women in bright colored dresses exited a shop. Charmaine, intrigued by what was inside, threw caution to the wind and jaunted across the road to investigate what the hullabaloo was about.

There she spied the most exquisite dress she had ever laid eyes on displayed in the window. It was ivory in color. The scoop neck was trimmed with crocheted floral lace. Beading adorned the collar, extending a few inches past the shoulders, and encircled the bust line. The three-quarter length sleeves were gathered with lace cuffs. A second layer of delicate lace draped across the left side of the dress. Captivated by the gown, Charmaine wanted a closer look. Wasting not a second, she pulled the large silver bar on the door of the boutique to look inside. When inside, she crept around the display window. She lifted the train of the dress to sneak a peek at the underside of the garment. The bodice had a built-in corset with a hook and eye closure in the back. Flattening the lace train to its original position, Charmaine released a wistful sigh.

She had always dreamed of wearing such finery for herself. However, where would she wear such an elegant gown? Most men in her fathers' circle wanted a demure, docile woman. Very unlike how she was. Many thought her too headstrong.

She had never considered herself as a candidate for marriage. Now, especially after this fiasco with Ali, the abduction…her father. She could almost hear the rumors flying about. Forcing the thought from her mind and feeling more melancholy than before, she decided to leave. As she reached for the handle of the door, a conversation caught her attention. Two whispering older women were gossiping about a fight. Charmaine inched closer to hear what they were saying. Charmaine found a large pink flower straw hat from a display. She placed it on her head, shadowing her face. With her back turned, she listened.

"…And that wild barbarian attacked two men. They were carrying guns no less."

"Where did you hear this?"

"It's all over the city. The police came and escorted several men out. Including the dark-haired barbarian. It all took place down the street. Some ladies were still out, and they happened to be nearby the scene of the crime when it happened. I believe it was at some rowdy tavern… The Stage and Rose is the name of it."

"You don't say?"

"Oh, I do, a demon he was." The eldest of the two women nodded with relish. "I heard his skin was the color of bronze; that he fought with the ferocity of a bear, and the speed of a god…"

"Where on earth do you suppose he came from?"

"From across the sea, I gather. Judging by his skin color and dark hair. I mean, where else do you find that type of man around?"

"Whoever he is or wherever he may be from, I hope he does not intend to stay."

"No room for those types of men in civilized society."

"Agreed." The two women nodded. They didn't have to mention his name for Charmaine to guess that they were most likely talking about Ali. There could only be one person who was bronze in color, hair black as night, and also a handsome demon. And who fought like a bear against two armed men. She placed the hat back onto its resting mount. The two ladies turned to find the large hat teetering on the display. Charmaine was already gone before they turned around.

She needed to find out exactly what happened that night at the Stag and Rose. And if those women were correct, Ali could be in big trouble. Retrieving her mare from the stable, Charmaine was off in a reckless gallop.

Her suspicions were confirmed when she spoke with the tavern keeper of the Stag. "Aye, the man you have described was here. Caused quite a ruckus, he did; he destroyed my tavern with no remorse. Foxed he was."

"Did he speak with anyone before the disturbance?" she asked.

"As I recall," the tavern keeper scratched his head in remembrance, "there were two men. One with blond hair and the other dark brown. They seemed to know him. He mentioned that he was none too happy to see them. He was pretty foxed, though. I'm not sure if he was serious; happens quite a lot around here."

Those men sound like Jasper and Oliver. Henrietta has them following us.

"Do you know where he might be now?"

"Oh yeah, the Bobbies came and carried 'em off. Took 'em right to the Yard. That's where you'll find him."

"Thank you, sir." Charmaine rushed away without a second glance.

"Hey! Don't I get a tip? Ahhh…" She was already out the door, so he dismissed the notion with a wave of his hand.

Charmaine arrived at Scotland Yard, escorted into an interior room by an officer. A short time later, she met with a guard who stood vigilant. "Excuse me, I'm searching for a man by the name of Ali Raza," Charmaine inquired in a hushed tone. "Third cell down," the man answered with a tone equal to her own. With a quick head nod, Charmaine walked a few steps before she stopped short to look for her bodyguard. There she saw him, a few steps away; she would recognize him anywhere, tall and handsome as ever, leaning against the bars of his cell. By the look on his face, Charmaine could tell he was not happy about his confinement.

"So, this is where you have been for two days." Charmaine called out with a note of amusement as she walked closer to him.

Ali swung around at the sound of her voice. "What are you doing here? Jasper and Oliver could be anywhere around here. They are probably following—wait. Did I not tell you to stay at the abbey?"

Charmaine shrugged. "If I had known you were prison this entire time, I would have come sooner to enjoy the sight."

"You speak in riddles, woman."

The sight of Ali behind bars gave her a strange sort of satisfaction, a sweet revenge for toying with her emotions the entire time. On the other hand, Charmaine had never been more relieved in her life.

The door creaked open, and he walked into the open room. "You have ten minutes," one of the guards interrupted out from the doorway.

"Look at your face, it's a mess! What the hell happened? And what's that horrid smell?" she clipped out before Ali could get a word in. "You reek of liquor and…never mind." Charmaine tried to avoid the smell by placing her hand in the air.

"The scent of man, my dear. Oh, and this little mishap, it's nothing serious."

"Nothing serious? You caused an uproar. If it weren't serious you wouldn't be in this mess. You have some serious explaining to do."

"Isn't it obvious? Just wrestling with old friends, nothing to worry about. And you need to go back where it's safe."

"Not until you tell me what is going on. Let's start with how Jasper and Oliver got into a fight with you."

"They're tracking us based on Henrietta's orders. The dragon lady more than likely wants us dead. So, we don't talk."

"What are you doing in London?"

"I'm on a mission. Like I said."

"What mission?"

"I'm not at liberty to say. Not to a civilian at least."

"You are now."

"I'm under strict orders not to do so. For your own safety."

"Oh, is that so? Well then, perhaps I can leave you in there until you do say."

The tick in his jaw indicated she struck a chord with him. "You wouldn't be able to survive a minute out there. Especially with Tweedle Dee and Tweedle Dumb out there, hot on your trail."

"You've already taught me everything I need to know. I survived fine before you, I can survive just fine without you." That was a blatant lie. She was utterly hopeless without him. She had already fallen for the man.

"Listen. I didn't want you to know because it could put you in danger as well. I'm on the hunt for someone more dangerous than Oliver and Jasper. More dangerous than Henrietta."

Intrigued, she said, "So. You knew."

He released a remorseful sigh. "In a way, I did. I needed a job as their carriage driver so I could get close enough...to track down my person of interest."

"Who might that be?"

"Break me out of here, and I can tell you more of what you need to know."

"After taking advantage of me? Then causing a fight at the Stag and Rose?"

"Oooh, you heard about that, did you?" He let out a surprising chuckle.

"This isn't a laughing matter. That bit of news is on every gossiping tongue in the city; you set off quite a scandal, I'll have you know."

"And I'll have you know, I did what I did in defense of your honor. As for the library ordeal, I apologized for it. It wasn't fair on my part. Yes. But you are a temptation in this mission—"

"What do you mean by that?" It was she who was caught off guard. Unaware that he ended the sentence.

"By what?"

"Me being a temptation. Is that true?"

Using his charm to get himself out of the mess, he arched dark brows. "Isn't it obvious? Look at you; you're ravishing. Beautiful. A fine prize for any man to marry. Especially gorgeous when you're angry."

Charmaine's heart nearly thumped out of her chest. "Seducing me won't convince me to break you out of there."

"It may help, though." Smiling, he tilted his head her way.

Damn, why did he have to smile like that? It was making her weak. "You think yourself clever, don't you?"

"In all honesty, you're still in harm's way. Those two puppets could be out there still anywhere, waiting to make their move. Waiting to kill you, or worse."

Charmaine was taken aback at the statement; the notion of Jasper and Oliver still at large changed the rhythm of her heart.

"Exactly. So, I need you to break me out of here if you're to have any chances of survival."

"How do you know that will happen?"

"I've seen it happen. I never want to see it happen to you, either."

"I'll think about it."

"Marry me."

"You are too bold."

"If the police discover what I am doing here, they will send me back to military prison in India."

"Where they are not forgiving."

Charmaine furrowed her brow.

"Time's up!" the prison guard bellowed.

"Are you absolutely serious, what you said? About being in prison in India?"

"I would never have said it otherwise."

"Come, Miss, it's time you be leavin' now." The guard was pushing her along.

"I'll think of something."

"I hope to God you do."

Chapter 14

Three days had passed since she left him in that cell. Two days she had busied herself on a plan to bail him out. A part of her wanted to leave him in there to teach him a lesson. Although the more she thought about it, she felt she ought to do the right thing. *This is ridiculous. There has to be a way out of this mess.* She was sitting alone at the long oak table in the dining hall, picking at the cold food with her fork. She sat there for a lengthy amount of time. She was too distracted to eat a morsel and too anxious.

What was she missing? Something was wrong. She closed her eyes to shut out the whirlwind in her mind. Try as she might, it was no use. Scoundrel or no, she had to make sure he was all right. Perhaps there was some way to convince the Constable to release him. Impossible though it may sound, she couldn't let him go mad in that cell.

Pushing her plate to the opposite end of the table, she rose from her chair. She retreated to her room to change, donning a pale blue day dress with a white collar a black polka dot ribbon. It was one of her more modest dresses. She went to the stable to saddle Honey, the horse she had befriended. She would make one more trip to town.

When she arrived at Scotland Yard, Charmaine bolted through the front door of the jail; she was blocked by two armed police officers. Stopping short in her tracks, she paled and shot into a panic. "Sirs, I'm here to see someone who was arrested three days ago. I need—" Charmaine stopped in mid-sentence "—I need to find him, please."

"This way," one of the officers spoke. And Charmaine was escorted to the interior office of the Yard. Once again led into the same room she had visited days prior, when the door opened to the interior jail something felt out of place. Charmaine peeked her head in between the two men to search for Ali. Her heart lurched in her throat. Ali was not there! The cell he once occupied was empty. Frantic, she dashed to the desk where the guard on duty sat.

"Where is he? The man who was in that cell three days ago, where did he go?" She pointed to the empty cell. The guard rose from desk to approach the young woman. He was a middle-aged man with graying hair, mustache, and hazel eyes, rotund in weight. He stood to his full height, peering down at her. "I'm not quite sure what you are talking about, Miss; it's my first day on duty this week."

"There was a man occupying that cell three days ago! Five-foot-seven, wavy black hair, brown eyes. He was here. Right here two days ago! Now he's not–" Charmaine couldn't finish. Covering her mouth, she could feel her heart plummet. She was on the verge of tears.

"Ahhh, him yes. It seems your man is a felon.

"What..." She was breathless, could hardly believe what was happening

"He's been sent elsewhere."

"Where? I demand to know."

"It seems something came up. There were two men who were also involved; they identified him. On the night of the tavern brawl, my report says…And I quote, they called him 'old friends.' Thus they proceeded to fight. He was arrested and brought to the station for two days." He placed the report down on the desk. "They moved him to a more secure location. He was released early this morning, so it seems."

Charmaine suddenly felt dizzy. She was too late. She left him here for too long; the statement that Ali told her was true.

"You have to take me there."

"I'm afraid I can't, Miss; I'm on duty at present."

Placing a hand on her forehead, she tried her best to remain calm. Charmaine couldn't think. Her head was spinning. "Where do I go?" Inhaling, then exhaling, she was trying to keep herself from fainting.

"I can't tell ya that, Miss. It's confidential. Considering he is a dangerous criminal. And a foreigner and all. You don't know what he's capable of."

"Sir, this is a matter of life and death; it is imperative that you release the dark haired solider who was in that cell; he is the only one who can trace two dangerous opiate dealers. My life, his life, as well as many others depend on the release of this man, and it's within your best interest I go and go immediately. Now, you have two choices. One, you will take me to where I need to go. Or, two, I will saddle up my horse and go myself. Either way, I have wasted enough time already." Seeing the earnest look in her eyes, her red face and the tears that threatened to follow, the guard gave in.

"I'll see what I can do. Don't go anywhere." He walked over to where a telephone box was hanging on the wall. He put the knob to his ear and began to dial a few numbers on the rotary. Charmaine paced back and forth to calm her nerves. It felt like ages until the man came back to tell her the news. "I'll have another guard escort you. I'm not supposed to do this, but this time I'll make an exception. Wait for the escort outside. He'll take you where you need to go."

Chapter 15

Shortly after leaving the office, Charmaine waited outside for the escort as the officer had requested. Now that she was outside, she was able to have a closer look at the majestic building, dwarfing other buildings that surrounded it. It was lined in redbrick, designed in the Portland stone style. Many windows adorned about every space available. Turrets protruded from all sides. Its small, yet steep roof sprouted a few small chimneys, and extra windows. The sheer size itself felt intimidating. An overwhelming sensation washed over her the more she examined the façade. She couldn't quell the whirlwind of emotions that spun through her. *I can't do this. Who rescues a man you hardly know out of prison? It's unheard of. It preposterous. It's something a proper lady would never think about doing.* Oh, bloody hell, who was she kidding? Everything up to this point was not proper. *I'm going to do this. As soon as I gather my courage… He would do the same for me.*

Charmaine placed her hands on her abdomen and sank to the curb. She wanted to do this. Yet, she couldn't resist the urge to run away—curl up in a ball on the bed back at the abbey or find her father for that matter. That would be far safer than risking her life to save an Indian soldier.

She never felt like this when she was around William. She had always been docile. Meek, was more like it. He had always been the one suggesting things. And she, a simpering female, blindly followed his lead without ever taking the initiative.

Come on, you goose of a girl. Ali needs your help. You cannot turn and run. Who knows what he is going through? He risked his life several times for you. It's time you rescue him. Ali had helped her more than once. Found her refuge, helped her with a new wardrobe when she had nothing. Taught her how to defend herself. Seduced her. And she fell for him. Banishing that thought from her mind, she couldn't let her fears get the better of her. As soon as he was free…he would be gone from her life. Forever. *Think…think…what would Ali do if he were here? He would more than likely charge through the building no questions asked, and then demand answers. Come to think of it. Oh goodness, I hope Ali isn't…*

Charmaine couldn't bear to think of it anymore. *I refuse to let my thoughts control me.*

"Excuse me, Miss," her escort called out, shaking her from her thoughts. "I do believe we should be going in now."

Charmaine swallowed the invisible lump in her throat, then looked up at the man. "Yes. Lead the way, sir.

~*~*~

Many voices echoed through the station. Muffled voices drowned out others; it was hard to differentiate who was calling whom. Charmaine could hear her name being called through the throng of voices. When her attention had been called back not only one guard, but two, joined her side.

"I'm sorry, what were you saying, sir?"

"You are a relation of his?" the second guard asked her.

"Ah…yes." Hesitation filled her voice.

"Follow me. This better not be some sort of scheme." The warning reverberated throughout her body. Offense replaced comeliness.

"Certainly not, sir." The first guard gave a nod to acknowledge her claim, then motioned in her direction to accompany him.

Charmaine followed the two armed guards through the grand station. Footsteps, along with the plethora of voices, echoed through the building. Everyone who was present looked up from their work to catch a glimpse of the woman who was walking with the guards. A round of mummers and whispers bounced off the walls. Charmaine paid them no mind as she continued to hold her head high. They passed through doors and long hallways for what seemed like miles, until they finally reached a door that read: "Authorized Personnel Only."

The armed officer reached for the silver keys and inserted one, skinny skeleton key, into the key lock. Thus, the escort continued to lead the small crew down a dark, narrow stone stairway, which brought them down to the basement of the facility.

Greeted by pungent odor as she passed through the door, Charmaine's apprehension grew with each step. She had never smelled anything like it. The old, damp, nauseating stench permeated every sense of her being. She didn't know where they were taking her, but she had to force herself not to retch. Wrapping her arms around herself to protect herself from the dampness that seeped within, the overwhelming feeling of dread consumed her.

"There." The escort stopped and pointed to the third cell down once they reached the bottom of the stairs. It took her eyes several minutes to adjust to the dark before she could approach. Proceeding with caution, as if she didn't want to disturb any unnatural force, she searched along the wall of empty cells. It reminded her of an abandoned circus stable. She spotted Ali sitting on the floor, head downcast and sullen. She would know that black head of hair anywhere.

"Ali." She breathed out his name and ran to him, relief flooding her. His hand clutched the bars of the cell. Tentatively, she reached through the bars to touch his face. "Oh, my word. What did they do to you?" Charmaine sank to her knees to meet him at eye level.

Bruised and disheveled, he looked up as if in a trance. "I'm dreaming, I have to be dreaming. Charmaine.

What are you doing here?" he managed through cracked lips.

"I'm here to rescue you."

"This isn't possible," he rambled incoherently. "My angelic Charmaine can't be here. Why do you torment me?"

"What are you talking about? I'm here. I—"

"You're too late," he interrupted.

She paled at the statement, taken aback. "What do you mean?"

"I've tried telling them who I am. They don't believe me. They have mistaken me for the hell-dog, Conroy. He must have forged his papers so I would look like the criminal. They're sending me back to India."

Charmaine removed her hand and sat straight up, covering her mouth.

"No…When?"

"Any given moment."

"No…" she whispered. Shaking her head, she placed her hands on the bars to hold herself up. "This can't be happening; it's all just a big misunderstanding. If I could talk to the police constable or the chief inspector and possibly have them—"

"It's no use, they won't listen."

"We have to do something!"

"There is nothing you can do."

119

A tear escaped Charmaine's eye. This man before her was about to be ripped from her. The same man who fought her abductors, who protected her, who cared for her. The same man who evoked something dormant within her, who drove her passion aflame by one simple touch. Frustrated, she was powerless to protect Ali when he needed her the most. She choked back a sob.

"Don't cry for me, you're much too beautiful. We had our time." Wiping the tear away with his dirty thumb, all he could do was stare as she trembled.

She caught his hand in hers, and her heart fluttered. "Why are you so afraid to tell me the truth?" Charmaine's voice broke.

"Losing you," was all he spoke. Charmaine, was taken aback by the remark. It was the first time Ali admitted his feelings to her.

She wasn't given time to reply. The first guard who had escorted her to the cell took her by the arm to help her up from the dirty floor, as the other unlocked Ali's jail cell. "It's time to go, Miss," he called to her.

The two guards took Ali by each arm to lead him out of the cell. A man, who wore the same uniform as the other two guards, only decorated in medals, joined them. Charmaine assumed him to be the police constable. He met the officers and Ali at the end of the corridor to usher him to his fate. All Charmaine could do was watch. Muted. Unable to form a sentence to save her protector. The world around her was crumbling. She failed.

Putting her hands to her head and shaking, she blurted out, "STOP!"

The three men and Ali turned in her direction.
"That man is my husband."

Chapter 16

Husband? She stood frozen in silence; the words had poured out of her mouth before she'd had time to think. Even Charmaine was in shock from her own statement. Husband…she could see Ali mouth the word right back to her.

"Did I say husband? What I mean is fiancé," she affirmed nervously.

She looked back at Ali for confirmation. He only closed his eyes and made a face.

"Now, that is a serious claim to be making, Miss." The police constable strolled back in her direction.

"Yes, I've gathered as much. And would you want a lady grieving so close to her wedding day, gentlemen?"

"Can you provide proof of such claim?"

"I-I-can, sir." She stammered her words out. "If provided enough time."

Charmaine could see Ali's perplexed facial expression. This wasn't going to be easy. *What have I gotten myself into this time?*

"Very well. You have forty-eight hours to provide proof that this man is your husband. Or whatever you claim him to be, or you'll both be in the klink."

"Yes, sir." Charmaine's heart hammered in her chest; she could feel the heat rise in her cheeks as she answered the constable. With a pang of relief Charmaine brushed past the guards, straight to Ali's side. She placed a hand on his cheek and looked to him with mirth. It was a victory, for now. Her hand moved to his shoulders, and she walked with her 'husband' out of his hellish situation.

~*~*~

The couple traveled on horseback to the abbey in silence. Recalling the past events, Ali was still in shock over what had just taken place in Scotland Yard. The journey felt longer, and more awkward than usual. The effect soon wore off as they reached the entrance of abbey, thus snapping him out of his trance. Ali had more time to broach the subject as soon as he found Charmaine was waiting with a basket of medical supplies.

"Husband…Fiancé…" Ali muttered to himself over and over. One hand covered his eyes.

"Of all the things in the world to say, that's what you came up with?" Sitting on the stone bench in the garden. Charmaine tended to Ali's bruises with a medicinal pumice made by the priest. She was concocting yet another plan for their newfound mess that she had created.

"I panicked. What was I supposed to say? You were the one who suggested I marry you when you were locked up."

As she wrapped his head in a bandage…he drew a sharp breath. "I didn't think you would take me seriously," Ali admitted.

"Besides," Charmaine continued. "I couldn't let them ship you back to some God-forsaken prison, even worse than the one you were in. If I had not claimed you as my spouse or relative, they would never believe me. The law would be more sympathetic to my fiancé."

"I suppose you have a point. But now we have a bigger problem to solve. Where are we going to find someone to do the ceremony? And they want documents. We are going to need a special license. That will not be easy."

"I've been living in an abbey for over the past few months. I could convince the priest, or he may know someone who may be able to do so. If we claim it's urgent I'm sure he'll consent," she finished as she pinned the bandage together.

"You do realize we don't have much time. What if this priest won't do it? What will we do then? Forge a document to prove our marriage?"

"If we have to."

You wicked woman.

"All right. What of the arrangements?"

"I'll figure something out."

"One more thing." He stopped her hand from patting his bruised cheek with a clean wash towel.

"Do you really want to go through with this? You do realize there is no turning back after this point. Do you really want to go through with this? It's a huge commitment." He could not have looked more adamant. "You do realize that once I marry you, there is no going back. You're stuck with me for life."

"Yes, I'm fully aware of the situation at hand. And I've come to the conclusion that I owe you."

"What do you mean by that?"

"That night, when you rescued me from the docks. And at the Stag, you protected my honor. Without you, who knows where I would be."

"I was just doing my duty." He placed a finger under her chin, tilting it up.

Charmaine crossed her arms. "You didn't have to. At least I can save you from a similar fate."

Ali stared at her. His mahogany eyes gleamed, studying the curvature of her lips; he wanted to kiss her for that statement.

He wanted her to say more. He wasn't satisfied with that answer; he wanted to hear her say she loved him or liked him just a little. "And you didn't need to save me."

"You would have done the same for me." She turned her head away.

"I suppose you're right." He gave a slight chuckle.

Chapter 17

The evening shadows descended upon the stone dwelling. Hues of pinks, oranges, purples and yellows painted the sky. Ali awaited in the garden; the primal spot for the couple. The irony of it all was. Ali had avoided marriage for years. Always believing the word was a curse rather than a blessing. Now, he found himself into the matrimonial responsibility to a woman he had no idea he had grown fond of. A slight smile crossed his face at the thought.

After all that they had been through, Ali felt compelled to find the perfect ring for Charmaine. He spent most time at the jewelers, determined, Ali would not give up until he found the perfect ring. But, everything he saw was either too big, too many jewels on it or not the right color for the occasion. Until out of the corner of his eye, he spotted a shimmer. Smaller diamonds within encircled the jewel, an oval cubic zirconia diamond. The petite silver band molded into a vine entwined together. An inlet of small studded flat crystals adorned the side to bring out its beauty. It was perfect, not overdone, yet giving it enough depth to stand out. To Ali, it was perfect.

He found his way to the garden shortly thereafter. Taking in some fresh air before the ceremony. He clutched the ring in his hand. He rose from the stone bench and placed the ring box in the pocket of his vest. With a jovial air, Ali rushed full speed from his resting place. Along the way, he came to the conclusion, he had been running from everything. And, it was catching up to him. It was up to him to make the change his life. *No more secrets. No more running. She deserves to know the truth, about everything.* With that notion in mind, Ali craved a bath for quite some time. After being in hellish underground prison and the arrangements for the ceremony. Ali relished the warmth that permeated his body. Taking his time in the soapy suds. Caressing his hardened hands with the soft sponge over indented lines, ripple and hair. Cascading droplets of water over his glistening taught body. Lathering his hands with the handmade Sandalwood soap. He made one final wash of his hair before the water turned tepid. He dried himself off. Then changing into finer clothing he had borrowed beforehand.

It took much convincing for the pair. Nevertheless, they had finally succeeded. A local priest, who lived nearby agreed to perform the nuptials. Examining the ring, his mind recollected the past events from the morning. He retold their story to the priest, an attendant Mary. So the two would not have the wrong idea on why he and Charmaine were getting married.

Ali, still engrossed in his thoughts, didn't even notice him when he almost collided into the aged man. "I beg your pardon, Sir." Ali rushed. "But I have no time to converse."

"Where are you going? The Ceremony is about to begin." He turned to face the priest.

"I'm going to find my fiancé." Ali called back.

Sitting at the vanity of her makeshift room. Charmaine fought with her hair, pinning the remaining tendrils of auburn into place. When she tried all she could, she gave up. Frustrated, Charmaine threw the hair-pin on the table in frustration catapulting it to the other end of the room. Burying her face in her hands Charmaine released a groan. *I'm not ready. There's no way I can do this.* Removing her hands she rose from the vanity in search of an escape route.

"I need to get out of here." When she was close to freedom, until her attendant Mary blocked her path. Mary, an aging woman. Petite stature with soft brown eyes, combined with brass-blond hair, accompanied by grey streaks. Her hair, assembled in a traditional Pompadour twist at the crown of her head.

"We're ready to begin Miss Radcliffe. Doing her best to remain calm, Charmaine smoothed any remaining wrinkles from the white dress. It wasn't the same dress she found at the shop she visited the afternoon prior to Ali's arrest. No, it's simpler.

Delicate lace short sleeves, low neck collar were trimmed with the same beaded accent. The straight lace material trailed down to her white slippers. She had found it amazing that she was able to acquire a wedding dress at all, given the amount of coin that remained.

Charmaine, for the first time since her mother had left, had no idea what she was doing. If her mother left some words of advice, maybe she would feel ready for this. Though, she was thrust into a life she had no time to prepare for.

"You look beautiful, Miss Radcliffe." Mary's words snapped her back to reality.

"Mary, you must listen to me." Turning to stand, bracing the aging woman by the shoulders as she spoke. "I cannot do this, I thought I was ready. But in all honesty, I am not. I have to get out of here."

"What on earth for?"

"Because I feel obligated to marry him; when he saved my life. Even though, I have grown to love him. Although, I feel it will end in heart ache-"

"Beg your pardon?'

"The man I am marrying. He saved my life, more than once. Now I feel guilt, because he believes he owes it to me; because I also saved him from a life or death situation. Which means. If I back out on this arrangement he can be taken back to his country. It would leave him humiliated, branded as a criminal. And I cannot let that happen because I think I'm falling in love with him. But, I am afraid. It is too good to be true." Mary stood back in mortification at the explanation Charmaine gave.

"You're not with child are you dear?" Mary asked with a quizzical stare, "He hasn't hurt ya at all dear?"

"I--No. On the contrary actually. He has been a gentleman this entire time. That's why I am afraid it's too good to be true, and I'll wake from this as if it were some dream. Although I feel it is very real."

Just then a loud knock came at the door. "Charmaine. I need to speak with you…" Ali's voice rang through from the other side, the time had come. "Charmaine, are you in there?"

"What do I do Mary? I cannot let him see me like this."

"Ahhh...ehh…"

"Go delay him, please. I'm not ready." Charmaine pleaded as the knocking grew louder.

Mary opened the door while Charmaine fled.

"Where is Charmaine? It's important that I speak with her."

"Sir, do you not know it is dreadful bad luck to see the bride before the ceremony. I cannot let you see her."

"Madam, I have no time to argue. Now I must find my bride. He forced open the door pushing past Mary, to only find an empty room.

"Where has she gone?"

"What do you mean Sir?"

Ali knew Mary was trying to waylay him. "Madam, I have no time to waste. Either you tell me where Charmaine has gone, or I will find her myself."

When Mary did not answer, that was Ali's confirmation to search out Charmaine for himself.

"Sir. Sir!" Mary continued raced after him. Ali did not hear as he walked to find Charmaine.

Charmaine heard Ali calling her name as his footsteps grew closer. She made her way out the side door of her room, which lead to the hall lined with stained glass windows. They were quite narrow. But, it was her ticket to escaping another mess.

Bracing her right foot onto one of the large oak benches, she lifted her left knee on the wide stone sill. She lifted the latch of the window and pushed the window outward. Charmaine fit herself through. As she secured freedom, she found that she couldn't move anymore. Trying to pull herself out; it was of no use. Charmaine was stuck!

"Oh no..." Wriggling back and forth, she tried to squeeze herself out. She heard the approaching footsteps. Charmaine let out a groan of defeat.

Ali's deep chuckle rang throughout the stone walls. "Stuck are you? How on earth did you manage to lodge yourself into that window?"

Still wedged in the tiny window, Charmaine felt humiliated. "Never mind how I got in here, get me out!"

"If I was in your position, I'd ask a bit more nicely." Treading onto the same bench. Ali took Charmaine by the waist. Shifting, Ali gave one more hard pull and Charmaine was loose. Tumbling backwards out of the window, falling onto the stone floor face first on top of him.

Ali quickly turned her in his arms and stared into her eyes. Charmaine felt the urge to kiss him. Or slap him. She couldn't decide.

"What do you think you were doing climbing out a window when we are supposed to be getting married?"

"I'm so sorry Ali, but I can't do it. I can't marry you."

"And why may I ask not? Even after that whole show you put on at the police station and in the garden? You're backing out?"

"I wouldn't make a good wife for you. I'm clumsy, I'm not prim or proper, nor subservient or demure. I speak my mind too much-"

"I know that. It's what I--admire about you."

"Whatever for?"

"You are a mystery I have yet to discover."
Charmaine pulled herself off of Ali to sit back on her knees. "I have nothing to offer. There are far more attractive, intelligent, and well-bred than myself. And my reputation is beyond ruined, no prospects..."

133

"That may be true. There are beautiful women out there who are attractive. But, I've been around my fair share of women, and I find most are selfish, care nothing for others. You are not like that, you have something no other woman has."

"And that would be?"

Ali didn't answer. Instead, he reined her into a heated, passionate kiss. Charmaine accepted as eager as he did, she had resisted enough. He didn't need to say it. She knew. She could feel a tear trickle down her cheek. This confirmed it. She was in love. Neither of them could pull away, nor did they want to. They both wanted to relish the moment.

It seemed as if forever passed before he broke from her. Misty eyed, she didn't even notice the tattered lace on her dress.

"Listen Jaan—*My Love*, I can't tell you how sorry I am that I hurt you, and caused you unforgivable sorrow. I shouldn't have seduced you, only to ask for professionalism after. That wasn't fair on my part." Brushing the stray tears away with his callous thumb." I can't promise you that I will be perfect. What I will promise you is that I will do what I can to make this work. To hell with what people might think."

"It sounds as if you said our vows already." She stated as she held back a sniffle.

"Consider it a trial run." He then leaned in to give her another kiss.

A clearing throat disrupted their encounter. "If there are no further distractions, we should proceed the ceremony." The priest said.

"Of course," Ali replied. The priest turned to walk away; Ali helped his bride to her feet, as they followed behind to the chapel.

Chapter 18

Mary finished repairing the tattered dress caused by the window just in time for Charmaine to walk down the aisle. A dream-like haze clouded her thinking. She hardly noticed the simple silver flower band Ali slipped on her finger. Though she saw him through the fog. And she had never seen him as clear as she had now. When the priest named the pair "man and wife" the foggy haze that was surrounding her brain had lifted. Regaining her composure, the kiss that they exchanged was soft, and delicate. Not at all like the kiss in the Library. This was humble.

Funny though it may seem. She had come to the conclusion that he became even more handsome when draped in candlelight. Somewhere along the way, an attraction had grown for the mysterious man she now called her husband. Yes, it is true, she was a married woman. Still, she had yet to wonder if he felt the same emotions as she did.

Charmaine packed the remaining of her belongings into a carpetbag. She paused to admire the sparkling diamond-gem adorning slender finger. She smiled softly as Charmaine noticed her reflection in the mirror. Could it be possible to love with someone she hardly knew? So much had happened in the last few months. It was hard to keep everything straight, although, she hadn't felt this happy in years. Surely she would able to adjust to this newly- wed life. What would Papa say? How will this predicament with Henrietta end? There were so many questions that they had yet to find answers.

However it was her wedding night and she forced herself to shake off all the unanswered questions. Charmaine had decided long ago that happiness was a state of mine, and right now she was happy. She now had a husband to consider. And nothing was about to stop her. Closing the carpetbag, she turned around at the room that had been her safe haven for weeks. Giving a silent farewell, Charmaine shut the door on this chapter of her new life. Walking out to the daylight, she noticed Ali's back to her. He seemed to be in deep thought reading a small piece of paper with numbers on it. She tapped him on the shoulder. "Ali, what are you reading?"

The sound of her voice jostled him from his thoughts. Turning to face her he replied. "Nothing of importance." Stuffing the paper into his shirt pocket, he proceeded towards her.

"A friend of mine has made arrangements for us to stay in his apartments while he's gone."

"Where has he gone?" she questioned taking the bag from here.

"He is traveling in Europe now. I wrote to him of our plight, and he insisted we occupy his home. He said it is the least he could do for our wedding gift."

Ali was starting to open up to her more and that

relieved her. Perhaps the more time they spent together, he would trust her more. If he would confide in her more, she wouldn't feel as alone.

Charmaine eyed the whitewashed stone cottage quizzically. It was a small home. Giving all the qualifications of a country cottage. Crimson shutters, white door, and flowers surround the stone perimeter. All the while preserving its cozy-like attributes. Conveniently, situated in a quiet street in Bloomsbury. In her opinion, it looked more like a dormitory, rather than a home. Her arm slinked around the crook of Ali's arm. He glanced in her direction. Ali seemed to notice her hesitation; he assuaged her worries in his nonchalant way when he spoke. "The exterior has much to be desired, although, the interior is much comfortable."

She looked in his eyes, "Do you think Henrietta will find us here?" her uneasiness was beginning to surface.

"I've been staying here for quite some time. No one seems to notice; it's secluded enough to keep you out of harm's way. There is no cause for worry."
He gave her one of his classic weak in the knees smiles. Her heart fluttered out of control, and she could feel color burn her cheeks." It's lovely."

"Shall we then?" He asked her.

~*~*~

The Firelight burned brightly in the master bedroom of the house. It had been so cold the last two nights. A fire was the only protection from the cold drafts that threatened the inhabitants.

Ali received his correspondences; one a telegram from the constable. It looked like he had a lead that could get him back on track to find Conroy. And there would be more information was on the way. But, his patience was growing thin. He didn't know how much time he had left. Three deaths had occurred during the week. The news has spread like wildfire all over the city. The tabloids had even caught wind of the opiate deaths.

Then, there were numerous death threats he had received towards Charmaine to consider. And himself. The words burned in the back of his memory.

"Further action will be taken. Unless Charmaine is brought forward." The other, was a note delivered to Scotland Yard directly, assuming it was from Henrietta.

He did not fear. He actually welcomed the adversary. Charmaine, on the other hand, was inexperienced. He could not risk her life. Balling the telegram in his hand, he inhaled a deep breath and gripped it in his fist to suppress the ache in his heart. Then in anger, he threw the letter it into the roaring fire.

Sure as hell Ali would be blackmailed somehow. It's happened before. The firelight illuminated his taut features. Sore from lack of sleep. He turned to his wife who was sound asleep in the bed a few feet away. Staring back into the flames with stoic features. His mission was clear. This ends now.

 Charmaine could see the figure in the dim light of the fire. She couldn't see clearly enough to get a good view, yet she could see the silhouette of a paper. *He has been standing by that fireplace for two days. What could he be possibly be reading?*

 Lying awake the entire time, only pretending to be asleep, she sought to study him unobserved. He looked so troubled and she had to repress the urge to climb out of bed to quell his worries.

 She'd do whatever it took to unravel what he is hiding. She rolled over in the queen-sized bed to find a comfortable spot. During that time he must have heard her, for he tip-toed over to his satchel. Charmaine could feel the weight of the mattress shift as her husband crawled in to join her. A warm, soft hand traced up her thigh, up to cup her bottom. It continued to trail up her side breast before sinewy arms molded around her. Charmaine felt a hardness press against her, and tickling sensation flood her core.

 She rolled over to prop herself up on her elbow.

She opened her mouth, to say something, only to find he had fallen asleep. Charmaine inched closer, she came millimeters away from his glossy lips. When she saw that the point of talk was moot. A hand pressed against his open shirt to feel his heart beat. Charmaine laid her head on Ali shoulder, the scent of Sandalwood & wood smoke filled her senses and she relaxed. She gazed into the face of her protector, now husband, until her eyes became heavy from fatigue.

Chapter 19

Sunlight glimmered through the frosted windowpanes in the bedroom where Charmaine dozed. Stretching the palm of her hand across the empty space of the bed that was once occupied, she took her time and lingered a bit longer than usual, enjoying the peace and quiet. The fire had died during the night and a chill permeated the air. The warmth she had felt when Ali was lying beside her had also faded. The smoke from the fireplace hovered in the air.

She adjusted her eyesight to the bright light of the morning. Charmaine took her time to rise from the warmth of the quilts. Propping herself up on her elbow, she toyed with the wrinkle of white cotton sheets. Until the warmth of the bed dissipated, forcing her to rise.

Swinging her feet over the side of the bed, she planted them on the chilled floorboards. The reaction initiated a protest for food from within. It was a steadfast reminder that she hadn't had anything to eat since she left the abbey. Charmaine placed a hand over her stomach, and thus removed herself from the frosty room.

For the first time in days, Charmaine felt a connection to the charming home. It was all on one level and furnished. It had all the amenities a home should have. Even a small steel heater bolted to the wall of the bedroom, as well in the study. Taking advantage, she opted to turn it on. She doubted if Ali knew how it worked. That's why he built a fire each night. A small smirk crossed Charmaine's lips at the reminder of the intimacy they'd shared the night before. Fierce, yet gentle, the affection that her new husband had shown her was something she didn't know she'd craved.

She glided her hands up and down her arms for warmth. The chiffon lace nightgown offered little protection against the bitter English winters. Charmaine searched the room for another source of warmth of protection. That was when she discovered a dark, wool wrapper draped over the end of the wrought iron bed. Sauntering to the end, Charmaine plucked it from its perch and draped it over her shoulders. As if by magic, the material offered her instant relief. Hugging herself, she proceeded to the kitchen for her breakfast. Upon passing through the house, she spied out of the corner of her eye the onset of her obsession: Ali's satchel. It was in the same place where he had left it the night before. It dawned on her that the mission had come to an abrupt stop. No word. No further inquiry of it.

Was he no longer in need of her assistance? Would he cast her aside now that he had what was he looking for? Would he take her back with him? Would she ever see her father again?

A sharp pang struck her heart. Charmaine closed her eyes as she placed a hand over her chest.

Lord, I hope not.

She was beginning to think the worst of what had become of her new husband.

Or was he leading a secret double life? Did he have a mistress? A wife somewhere? He had told her it was not usually common. But he could have been teasing her.

Was he? I'm letting my bad thoughts cloud my judgment. It was probably nothing, Charmaine; don't jump to conclusions just yet.

Her mind kept wandering to the satchel in the bedroom. Try as she might, she did everything possible to banish it from her mind. *It isn't right to snoop in other people's things...But if his thing, were now your things it's perfectly justifiable, right? Wait. I can't take advantage of him like that. I need him to trust me.*

Charmaine felt sorely in need of clearing her head, and she rotated her index and middle fingers on her temples in a clockwise motion. Charmaine cleared the small table of the unused dishes in the washtub, and braced herself against the edge. Her mind was too full of worry to eat anything.

Mindlessly, she strolled carefree through the house. Her fingertips floated on each object as she passed by. She found her way to the small study and glanced up at the small mantel clock. 11am.

There, across the room, was a tall oak bookcase. In it was a collection of literature. Among the work was that of Charles Dickens. *A Christmas Carol* caught her eye. Crossing the room in two short strides she bent to ease book from its encasement. In no time she had immersed herself, not giving a thought to anything else.

~*~*~

The mantel clock above the fireplace chimed three times, the loud *ting...ting..ting* bidding Charmaine to wake from her slumber. Her eyelids fluttered as she removed a stiff arm from under her neck. She had fallen asleep on the settee of the study with the open book on her lap, one hand resting on top. The hour reminded Charmaine that the time for afternoon tea was far-gone, as was lunch. *He still isn't back yet? What was he doing all this time?* He had been coming and going quite a bit. Would her suspicions be relevant? She wanted, no, needed, some sort of proof that her claim was all in her head.

"I'm sure there is no harm in taking a little peek. After, I will put everything back where it was, and there will be no harm done. Right?" Charmaine tried to convince herself. *No.* She wanted Ali to trust her. That was doubtable if that were to happen anytime soon. Charmaine made up her mind once and for all. She placed the book down beside her as she rose from the settee, and sailed into the bedroom where the satchel lay.

Once she had the satchel in her hands, it took several moments to gather her courage to open it. With a deep breath, she lifted the flap. Inside was a stack of papers. Placing the bag on the bed, she examined the contents inside. What Charmaine found was, in her opinion, worse. The death threats. "...*hand over the girl, and no harm will come to you.*"

The file: "Jonathan Conroy...D.O.B. 21st June 1880."Jonathan Conroy? *Jonathan. The man who was assisting Henrietta.*

Then came the tabloid clipping. "Three deaths in a span of seven days...all produced the same cause of death dose of opium found in the victims. No leads as of yet...No leads? Henrietta is the one they need," she to herself.

"What the bloody hell?"

The discharge letter...For suspicions of Desertion. One Lt. Ali Raza failed to return to base for a full report. Due to your actions on 7th February 1910, you are hereby discharged..."

Then she heard his voice, the voice of her new husband. Charmaine was caught red-handed.

"Didn't anyone tell you that it isn't right to pry into someone's personal belongings?" Ali's tone was flat, and cold.

"What is this? What is going on?" Charmaine breathed in a huff, her cheeks painted red from anger. She had his papers gripped in her hand, waving them in the air.

"It's none of your concern," he said as he inched in Charmaine's direction.

"None of my concern? When it involves me, how is that not my concern?" The pitch in her voice rose a few octaves. "I don't even know who the hell I married. Are you a convicted felon? A murderer? Have you a mistress on the side? Or are you married to another, perhaps?"

She continued to chatter on angrily, until Ali decided to catch her by the shoulders. Swooping down to plant a heated kiss on her lips in hopes to assuage her anger, Ali savored the contact for a few precious minutes. Until Charmaine shoved him away.

"NO! That will not work on me, not this time. I demand the truth. Are you, or are you not, dealing opium?"

"Of course not." Ali bit out.

"Then why are you always coming and going? Why were you there that night I was abducted?"

Teetering on the edge of control, Ali took a deep breath to speak. "I told you once before…"

"Right, on a mission to find who tried to kill you." Charmaine finished the sentence in a mocking tone.

"Yes. I was there that night, undercover as Henrietta's driver. She promised to help me find the man I seek. I was searching for Jonathan Conroy, with no luck. When I found some answers in the underground, I asked for information about him; she agreed on the condition I become her carriage driver. It was another ploy, no doubt."

Ali once again regained enough control to continue his thoughts. "I had him, too. I had to hide the truth from you because I felt that was the only way to protect you."

"Protect me?!" Charmaine forced the word out.

"From your drug-peddling boss, Henrietta Flint, and her gang of thugs that's who. Are you so naive that you can't see that your darling Henrietta is a drug lord? She will kill us both. Do you realize that? How do I know you're not involved with the two, and the plan you were concocting went awry?"

"How can you say that?" She looked into his eyes with reserved calm, yet on the edge of tears.

"Well?" Ali shot back.

Charmaine stood straight and tall, and forced herself to swallow the lump of emotion stuck in her throat. "I'll have you know I had no such doings. And, I had the situation completely under control." She spoke with poise.

"Under control?" Ali scoffed at the statement. His hand stroked the shadow on his chin. "As I recall, Mrs. Raza. Tied down by two grown men, twice your size. You were about to be backhanded and fed opium against your will. You sure had the situation handled quite well. In all honesty, if I hadn't come to your rescue, you'd be—" He couldn't bring himself to finish the sentence. He turned away from her. Sickness rose in his stomach, and he covered his mouth to prevent further action.

"All right." Closing his eyes, he inhaled a breath. "You mentioned once before you saw a large man with Henrietta that night. You need to tell me exactly what happened. Right before Oliver and Jasper abducted you. What did you see?" He knew the answer already. He needed to hear it from her to confirm his suspicions. "What did he look like?" Ali rubbed his closed eyes. "Every single detail you saw that night, and don't leave out a single thing."

Charmaine released the papers she held in her hand, and let them float down to the chair. "Henrietta called him…Jonathan. He was assisting her, from what I assume when I overheard their conversation that night. I was bringing Henrietta the money we made from our sales. So she could add it to the income of the business. I saw the large man standing behind her, as if he were protecting her. Henrietta mentioned opium, and that the gentlemen would receive what they paid for. I'm assuming, she tried to persuade the men to buy her inventory. So he could sell it to the degenerates of society. To make a profit." Waving her hand as she turned her head away from him, Charmaine released the breath she held in to continue what she remembered. "The man thought Henrietta was cheating him out of the deal. I had no idea the shop was struggling. My father and I are struggling as well, after months of searching for work to help us survive. Honestly, if I had known the true motives to her scheme, I would have turned back in an instant."

"Of course." Ali began to mutter to himself, his hands on his hips he turned away. "It makes sense that he would hide in a large city. No one would know where he is. He was more than likely sent by a higher authority to do their dirty work to sell that opium to a new clientele. The underground would be a prime spot for his dealings, too. Jasper and Oliver more than likely figured out that the opium Henrietta dealt was not pure." When Ali looked back in her direction, he could see her face was still flushed with anger, with tears threatening to spill from her eyes. Ali could feel his heart skip a few beats. A beautiful woman like Charmaine shouldn't have to scavenge for work. How did it come to that?

"I must have made a noise." She broke his reverie, "because, before I knew what was happening, the door flew open. Jasper and Oliver grabbed me before I had the chance to escape. In all honesty, I would never have sought your help if I could have prevented it. I'm not as naïve as I look so, in the future, please don't question my character. If you trust your own wife, or anyone for that matter, then what was all this for? Did I only marry you to save your sorry arse?"

Ali combed his fingers through his hair; frustration wracked his nerves. He spoke with every ounce of strength to soothe his heated temper. "I ask every question I can involving this mystery, feelings be damned. Not to forget, you asked me for help in the beginning. I used every shred of coin I had to house, feed, and clothe you, to care for you in every way I know how. Now, because of your venture, I

151

have gone completely broke from it. I've been out during the mornings on watch in the frigid air so, God forbid, Oliver and Jasper do not discover us. Not to mention delivering our special license and papers to Scotland Yard, as proof of our sham of marriage. I am exhausted from this entire endeavor and I haven't even come close to finishing what I set out to do. So, I'll ask you, Mrs. Raza, not to question my character as well." His words shot like daggers through his own heart. He had spoken the word "sham" aloud. Ali winced at the pain that crossed his wife's face, and turned away. His words clearly affected her more than he thought.

Ali's anger clouded his thinking, once again. His chest tightened. "Charmaine… I didn't mean…" This time with more emotion in his voice: "I'm sorry. I didn't mean for it to sound that way." He walked to her. "There is something you should know. Yes, you do deserve the truth." He spoke as he inhaled. "But, I warn you. It is not what you want to hear."

"Why are you so afraid to trust me?" Charmaine's voice was more sincere.

"Because I am afraid you won't see me the same way as before," Ali finally admitted. "It's a past I've tried to run from. To forget. The scars run much deeper. But first, you must swear in absolute secrecy that you will keep it to yourself until I am finished with my business. And do not interfere."

"Yes," he heard his wife whisper.

"You have no need to have any fear of me, Charmaine; I have given you my word to protect you until the end. And I mean it in every sense of the word."

Chapter 20

"In order to understand, you must know what happened in the beginning. I was a young boy of ten. My mother, father, and I were traveling on our way on a pilgrimage with some of our kin. We traveled for several weeks through miles of desert. A day away from our journey's end, a band of marauders attacked us from out of nowhere. "I could see black shapes on the hilly sandy dune through the blistering sun. Then they came closer. I stayed still and held onto my mother. Then they began raining down upon us, swords and all.

"I didn't understand what was going on. I watched in horror as the men slaughtered my kin. Everyone was dying, defenseless. We were at the mercy of those bastards. I could hear the screams of the women—the hoof-beats of the horses as they charged past.

"A boy of thirteen came up to me. His hood was down, covering his face, so he figured I could not see his face before I died. My mother, with whatever strength she had left, threw herself on top of me to save my life. In the darkness, I could hear the ringing of the sword he pulled out from the sheath. I thought it was over for us.

155

"A whistle sounded in the distance. Sheathing his sword, the attack never came. All was quiet. The marauders had left. It was over. The boy walked away, sparing my life. And my mother's. When I crawled out from under my mother, I looked around to find any survivors, for help. My cries were in vain; they'd murdered everyone around me. My father, my kin. Even my faith." The final word he choked out. "Except for my mother."

"With the materials left over I built a makeshift pallet, to carry her from the heinous scene. Hours passed. I was able to find refuge in a cave. There, I was able to bind her wound, and wait until further recourse. After a day of traveling I made it to a small town, where I found help. Mother found the care she needed, but the aftermath of the attack left her scarred for life. I never heard her speak from that day on.

"After the incident, I lived with my grandmother and my remaining family until I was of age. I joined the army. I fought, trained in the art of the sword, and in fighting skills until I became the best the military had to offer.

"I killed and added to a high death-toll I am not proud of. I thought it would help to mask the pain I was harboring, to drown the memories. I vowed, when I was old enough, I would find that boy who stole everything from us. And I would take my revenge for what I had lost.

"I came home after months of active duty. I found my aunts had arranged a marriage for me. My reputation grew and soon caught word.

"The woman came from a respectable name and wealth. After months of courtship, I broke off the engagement. She grew ostentatious, selfish, and egotistical. Perhaps it was resentment that grew, or I was being selfish. Whatever the case, I could not bear to be around her any longer. Naturally, my family was furious. With our families joined I could have the life I deserved, never want for anything. And they could have the life they wanted. I didn't care. All my family wanted was wealth, prestige, and praise. And they were using me to get it. I don't know what was worse: Maya's behavior or my family's greed. In time, I became indifferent. I left. I haven't been home in ten years.

"Before traveling to England. I was in charge of a platoon of men. We were fighting the British military in the Thar Desert. Britain wants full and absolute control of our textiles and the lands that produce them. The opposition assumed, after all the years of war, that our resolve would weaken. They assumed we would succumb to their demands.

"When the battle was over, I was discussing further plans with my second in command. I have no recollection after fainted. Although, I believe I was rendered unconscious. Afterward, I was thrown out into the unforgiving desert. I was left for dead. It was by chance that a caravan happened to be crossing through; they rescued me. The people, they cared for me. They did not

157

know who I was. They nursed me until I was strong enough.

"It was the elder of the caravan who gave me some information on the dagger I showed you. Now that I am here, I am determined to find the man who tried to have me killed. That man is Jonathan Conroy. The man you have mentioned is the same man I am hunting. Although, that is not his real name. It is an alias he is using to protect himself. And I suspect he is the one responsible for the opium deaths throughout the city. I also have reason to believe he is the one who is behind sabotaging me. So I would go to prison and he would be able to continue his dirty work. It would pin his crime on me, sending me back to India, disgraced. He is determined to ruin me. Now that you are tied to me, he is relentless. He and Henrietta will kill you without a second thought.

"He is a ruthless, vicious, self-centered man. And will do anything to gain what he wants. Even if it means killing innocents. A man like that is heartless."

Charmaine could only stare into the fire in the fireplace. She was solemn, trying to absorb the story.

"Do you see now why this mission is so important? I—I can't let any more innocents die. Not while I can prevent it. It makes sense that he would hide in a large city. No one would know where he is. Then, I had him. It was the night you were abducted. I had a choice. I could take him down and receive my justice, or save you. As you can see, I chose the latter. I accepted your offer of being your bodyguard because I figured I could use your knowledge of the city."

She looked to him. "Why not go back to Henrietta? Demand that she turn him over to you?"

"If I were to go back to her, she would kill me if she doesn't get what she wants."

"Me," Charmaine muttered.

"The threats that were sent to you indicated that no harm was to come to you. But that was no guarantee. I couldn't risk it."

She put a hand on his face, turning him to her.

"Is that what you have been hiding from me all this time?" she managed to say.

"Yes," he whispered. He looked her straight in the eye; she pulled him in for a kiss. He accepted. The kiss was soft but unyielding. Charmaine pulled away to speak. "I don't know how I can ever thank you. I am so sorry. It was my fault you lost your chance. I had no idea."

"You couldn't have known." He cast his head downward. She placed her hand in his as a comfort. "Although, in a way, I am glad for it."

"Why?"

"Because it gave me the opportunity to find you. I never knew it would be like this. I never intended to hurt you, or put you in danger. I might have wanted to tease you, but that teasing turned into something I couldn't control." She turned away, smiling, and blushing a bright hue despite the glow of the fire.

My God, she's beautiful when she smiles. He turned his head.

She broke his concentration. "There is nothing that we can do now. Despite everything that has happened. Your father, uncles. All the others—they would never want you to kill anyone to avenge them. Revenge is never the answer; it only breeds more hate. You have been through so much, it's understandable that you harbor so much pain. Anger only causes more hurt. You shy away because you don't want to hurt anymore or hurt anyone else in the process. But please know, the more you push others away the more you hurt them."

He rose from the settee and walked over to the fireplace, placing one arm on the mantel. He took a few minutes to absorb her words.

She's right. Although, too much has happened to turn back now.

"You have such a kind heart, *Pyaar.* Love. I am so close to finding him. I can't give up what I set out to do. He has hurt too many already. Now that you are involved he'll come for you, too. I need you to be here where it's safe; there is no telling what he may do."

"No! You can't be serious. I am going with you. It's my fight, too—"

"Out of the question." He came back to her, crouching down to her, placing his hands on her knees. "You are already in danger with Henrietta. I saved you that night because I couldn't let them hurt you." He cupped her face. "I can't involve you anymore. I don't even want to think of the outcome if—" Brushing a stray lock of hair behind her ear, he continued. "When I bring him to justice…" He sucked in a breath. "You may not like what you see if I revert to a part of me I am not proud of.

"I don't care. I can't lose you." Her heart was in her throat.

"I will come back to you." *If I make it back.* "I'm not that easy to kill, remember? You have given me strength to keep going this entire time. I need you to be strong for me still. I can't worry about you when I am fighting him. Please. Wait for me."

"You have saved my life, protected me when you needn't, saved my reputation. And even now, you trust me enough to give me a glimpse of yourself. I could not be more thankful for what you have given me. Would it be too much to ask to be your everything? Your hope, your comfort? To be your happiness?"

He broke the hold she had on him. Taking her by the arms, he helped her to stand.

"Do you still not see? You have been my solace and my chaos all at once—my poison and my remedy. You drive me to madness at every turn, and there is no help for it. I've tried running from it, but it's no use. And it's killing me inside. And you have been here all this time.

"Can't you see I'm in love with you?" He released a breath. "It's been you this entire time, and I'm not running anymore." Taking her in his arms, he enveloped her with all the pent-up feeling he had held back.

His hands cupped Charmaine's face, cradling her face with his fingers. Softly, ever so gently, he brushed her lips with his. Time stood still, everything she was thinking evaporated.

He's been in love with me this entire time, and I had no idea.

She wanted to breathe, but found it incredibly difficult. Dizziness overcame her senses. Her hands climbed up his shirt collar, clutching the soft fabric for support. It had been an indication to pull her in closer, deepening the kiss between them. Charmaine could feel his hands trailing down to her bottom, grasping. Rising beneath his touch, the warm tingle was returning, pooling in her nether regions.

His hands moved to the back of her skirt, loosening the clasps, and allowing it to pool to the floor beneath her feet. She didn't stop him this time; she had no reason to hide. He loved her. Ali continued to trail the feather-like kisses down her neck. A soft sigh escaped to the response. With one kiss, his touch, Charmaine was paralyzed. She was helpless from within. The white cotton buttons of her blouse were coming undone. She didn't even notice as Ali tore it free from her heated body, to stand before him, clad in her lace bodice and corset.

She shivered beneath his touch. He caressed the curvature of her hips, bringing his hands up to circle the lace of the bodice. He moved his hands up to untie the blue ribbon holding the material together. Her heart hammered at the thought of her exposed breasts protruding before him.

Charmaine, oblivious to the fact that her corset had already discarded to the floor, could feel his hot gaze upon her. She stared up to meet him. Suddenly, she felt sheepish. Smoldering with desire, he spoke with a ragged breath.

"My God."

Completely nude before him, Charmaine felt the heat of embarrassment. He calmed her nerves as his hand reached up to her cheek, smoothing her auburn hair. A kiss planted on space between her ear and cheek. "Don't hide yourself, *Dil Rubo*. Sweetheart. You're perfect," he whispered in her ear as he removed the pins from her tresses. A wave of silk tumbled down her back.

The warmth that he projected gravitated to her swollen lips. He guided Charmaine's trembling hand to his half-open shirt. Grazing his fingertips to her forearm. She was fascinated by what lay beneath. Slowly unfastening each individual button. She could feel his need growing under her touch. Soon, his sinewy frame was in full view as she parted the shirt. Charmaine pulled away to see. Opening her eyes, she was mesmerized by the taut muscle glowing bronze in the firelight. Her heart hammered in her throat with each caress against the smooth skin. He was an Adonis. Sculpted by time and hardened by war. She had never seen anything so glorious. He must have sensed unease because the hold he had on her broke. Removing the loose material, he discarded the shirt to the floor. Until only his trousers remained.

163

Picking her up, he carried her to the bed, bending to capture her lips with his. Encircling her arms around his entire width, Charmaine had been waiting for this for so long, for Ali like this. Without restraint or consequences.

She pulled him to her for a full kiss, running her hands through his soft, ebony locks. He reciprocated by gingerly pushing her back onto the billowy quilts, climbing on top of her. Roving her neck, trailing kisses down to her chest.

His hands found their way to her lush breasts. Cupping one in his palm, Ali began to massage with urgency. The motion caused a low moan of pleasure to escape her. Especially when a taut nipple found itself in the hot cavern of his mouth. Tormenting her, teasing it with his tongue. She hardly noticed when he moved swiftly to pay homage to the second breast. The sensation that tingled between her legs began to throb. And she squirmed under his touch. Removing himself, a hand trailed down her thigh, beckoning them to part. There was the honey pot.

Sinking her head into the feather pillows, his finger found its goal between the damp curls. Slick, ready. Caressing the folds of her sex, she released a soft moan, arching from the shivering sensation.

Closing her eyes, breathing seemed like the only valid response.

"I can feel your need, *Pyaar*. You're so ready. It is torture for me."

She felt the weight lift off her, and she opened her eyes. Charmaine could see her husband unbutton his trousers, discarding them to the floor, giving her a better view of his full erection. As if by magic, it grew. Standing before her, Charmaine could only stare in amazement.

"This is what you do to me. I have lost all control." His breath was rasping.

Propping herself onto her elbow, she gave a coy smile. She waved her index finger back and forth, bidding him to come to her. Bringing herself to a sitting position, it would be her turn to turn Ali defenseless.

Taking a trembling hand, she grasped his hard shaft. His hand once again caressed hers, instructing her. Guiding her caress up and down the smooth shaft. Increasing the sensation within. She saw him tilt his head back, releasing a groan.

"Slow, love, slow." His voice was ragged. The coy Charmaine had turned into a seductress. An impish smile crossed her lips, knowing the sweet torture she was causing.

"Kiss me," Charmaine called in a sensual voice against his ear. Her command was fulfilled when a fiery kiss captured her lips.

Ali overtook her, bearing her down upon her. Trepidation hit, followed by excitement. Remaining calm, she closed her eyes to welcome what was to come.

"You're going to feel pain, but I'll do my best to not hurt you. Move with me and the pressure will subside. Do you trust me?"

"Yes," She squeaked out.

He put his full weight upon her. Maneuvering her leg around his torso, guiding the soft shaft inside her. Moving slowly at first, he wrapped his bronze, solid frame around her body to prevent her from flinching as she cried out from the pain when he penetrated.

Her breath caught in her throat. Her heart began to pound out of her chest. His firm hands grasped her naked buttocks, suddenly driving his hard shaft into her. A loud gasp escaped. It was silenced by gently crushing his lips to hers. He rocked gently back and forth, gaining a little momentum with each stride. Pain filled her insides. Glorious vibrations took over, bringing her to the heights of climax.

Faster and faster and faster, until her breath came in shallow raspy gasps. Moving with his thrusts, she could feel the stimulating euphoria that was building.

"Oh! Yes!" and a sharp intake of breath. Spasms wracked her body as she released. They paused for a few moments, basking in the afterglow of their lovemaking. Their bodies and souls were united.

He moved off her to lie on his forearm next to her. He clasped his hand in hers and spoke.

"I hope I didn't hurt you."

"Not as bad as I thought. It was…exhilarating. Is it always like that?"

"Usually it's better."

She smiled and looked at him, then closed her eyes to sleep.

Ali lay there, still wide awake, basking in the

beauty that had transpired between them.

Chapter 21

"*Pyaar*." His nimble, strong hand glided up Charmaine's shoulder.

"Hmmm." A small sound emanated through the stillness. They lay in bed, tangled in the sheets, basking in the afterglow of their lovemaking.

"Have you been a seamstress for long?"

"For a while. Why?" Charmaine's soft voice answered.

"Have you ever thought of opening your own dress shop? This may not be the best time to ask this. But, you could use your knowledge of design to make a good profit." Ali propped his hand under his head.

"It is not as simple as that." Goose pimples formed where Ali's hand once roamed. "There are…restrictions for women. I can't even make my own earnings without a male figure handling the finances. It's not that I'm not able. It's the way of life for a woman. I've always dreamed of having my own dress shop. To have people admire my creations. Although I begin to realize, it isn't in the lot for me."

"I'm sure your mother…" Ali began.

"My mother is no longer with us." The words escaped her lips as she wrapped her arms around her torso.

Memories flooded back to her childhood. Of her mother; so loving, caring.

The sunlight flooded the dayroom where Anne Radcliffe sat. Situated in a round, cushioned arm chair, she occupied her time with needle point, while humming a soft tune. A small girl at the time, Charmaine played with a porcelain doll on the large circle rug. She lifted her head to the sound of her mother's humming. Anne was beautiful, a halo of light illuminated her features; high cheek bones, a petite nose, and warm brown eyes. Her chestnut hair was neatly styled her hair in a pompadour bun—a loose coiffeur assembled at the top of her head. When her mother smiled, it seemed as if music filled the air. She was most certainly a sight to behold. That memory would be with her forever. It was the only memory she had left of her mother. Charmaine squeezed her eyes tight as she winced from the painful thoughts.

"I'm sorry; I should not have brought it up. I assumed she was alive."

"She is alive. She left us when I was a young girl…"

"Do you wish to talk about it?"

She was quiet for a few moments. "It happened several years ago. Our family was well off. I had a good education, and many possibilities for suitors, finery. Everything a girl could want. My father was a successful merchant, shipping and trading goods from all over. He was always consumed with work, spending days at a time there; we hardly saw him. My mother was a beauty," Charmaine continued as a tear escaped her eye. "She had an affair with my father's lawyer. I am uncertain of the whys or the how's, she probably felt neglected for far too long. So, she left, without as much as a goodbye. She did well to put on a brave face. But I had this feeling she was only playing her part in front of me until the opportunity came to take her leave. I was sixteen when it happened. After the incident, my father grew depressed. He neglected the business; he turned to drinking, and the business fell into failure. My father later realized his mistake. But, by the time he could fix it, it was too late. The banks would not even help. 'Too much of a labiality' was their excuse. We had no choice but to sell our possessions, all my dresses, all our furniture. Anything to keep us afloat. In the end, I had to dispel my education.

"Then, William Tate happened. He was handsome, charming, charismatic…a cur. Things became worse from there. He claimed he wanted to help my father rebuild what he had lost. We were so relieved to have help, taken in by his charms. After a few months of courtship, he asked my father to see the accounts. My father refused. When Tate didn't get what he wanted, he persisted. An argument broke out between my father and him. In the end, he came to me, and convinced…well, he seduced me… into searching for them. I was so enamored with him, I trusted him. So, I relented. Little did I know it would lead to our ultimate downfall." She choked on the last sentence.

"He had no intention of staying. He had no intention of marrying me. I never saw him again. He took everything from me—from us. He destroyed what we had left. In the end, all I had left was a broken heart. Not a penny to my name, and ruined. I was never able to find a suitable husband after that—especially not with the rumors. Who would want a silly girl who had nothing to offer? We salvaged what we could. To keep creditors at bay, I needed to find work. If I had known about Henrietta, I would never have asked. I worked at the shop as her assistant. She took pity on me. Since she was a schoolmate of my mother's, I was unsuspecting. The money I made kept us afloat. But now, I don't know what to do. I'm only hoping my father is doing everything in his power to stay out of trouble. If only we—I—saw through his ruse sooner, this whole mess would never had happened." Ali moved closer to her, holding her tighter as she choked back a sob.

"*Jaan*." He spoke softly. "You couldn't have known at the time."

"You must think me a fool," she mumbled against his chest.

"I could never think that. You didn't know. It was a hard lesson, but you know now." He smoothed his hand through her hair.

"Anyone can be a skilled conman if they can play their cards right. You just were so taken with the man that you failed to see through him. You can't keep blaming yourself for that."

"But it will haunt me for the rest of my life."

He said nothing, lying there in silence. He drew her

chin to kiss her lips in the glow of the fire.

~*~*~

Ali gazed upon the sleeping woman who lay beside him. Still, serene, unsuspecting. Her hair fell in amber waves, blanketing her face, the right hand touching her cheek. Ali clutched his chest in an attempt to quell the ache that manifested.

So beautiful. So innocent. I'm sorry, Mera Dil Ruba. *I can't say goodbye to you while you are awake. But you wouldn't understand. Even if I explain, you would do everything possible to prevent me from going.* He released a heavy sigh to relieve the pain. *This is something I have to face on my own. I desperately wish we could have met under different circumstances. Maybe then, I could have loved you longer.*

"I always want to remember you this way," he spoke softly to her, followed by soft words into her ear as he kissed the top of her forehead to bid her a farewell. He lifted his head, opened his eyes, and noticed Charmaine's' lips twitch into a slight smile. With one last pull on his belt, Ali secured the gun holster and strode out the door. Down the stone staircase into the bitter, frosted afternoon to where the entire confrontation would end.

~*~*~

The sound of the door resounded through the empty house. Charmaine came alive, and moved at a snail-like pace to stretch an arm to the left side of the bed. Only to discover it empty.

Charmaine cracked her eyelids open and pulled the white sheet up to cover her naked chest, positioning herself to scout the room. But, there was no trace of her husband anywhere. Even the red, oval chair that housed his satchel sat empty in the corner. With one fluid motion, the sheet molded around her body. And Charmain removed herself from the vacant bed to wander the small manse. Her heart hammered in her chest as every nook and cranny remained empty. Even the small kitchenette remained as it was. Empty. After a lengthy time, Charmaine realized silence was her companion. She sank to the floor in defeat, her hand covering her mouth to prevent any noise escaping.

No… Out of the corner of her eye she saw a crumpled up piece of paper by the fireplace. *Unless…* She could feel her body inflate with air once more.

Of course…

Ali walked into the dusty, abandoned warehouse, where he'd rescued Charmaine six months earlier. Despite the dim expanse of the facility, he could make out the silhouette. Projected by the lighting that stood by the wooden table, the voice sounded.

"I thought you would never come," the voice spoke. Ali continued to move forward with cool reserve as he came face to face with him.

"It would have been fortunate for you if I hadn't, Rajesh. It was a good chase while it lasted. Now, I tire of this cat-and-mouse game."

"*Oui* oui. What's with the attitude, Bhai? Are you not overjoyed to see me?" his comrade questioned.

"I am not your brother, and I will be more than overjoyed when I'm rid of you," Ali continued, his voice laced with dangerous ire. "It is a shame you didn't let the desert claim my life like you planned."

"Surely—"

"Don't play, Rajesh. I know it was you who staged the attack in the Thar," Ali interrupted hotly. "The Kindjal dagger you left behind; it's custom-made. When the Nomads rescued me in the Thar it was recovered, along with my half-dead corpse. Their chieftain told me its origins; I could only surmise that it came from you, since you told me of your exploits when stationed in Ankara. Not to mention this dismissal letter," Ali added as he tossed the torn envelope onto the dusty table.

"Is that all?" Rajesh implied, his muscular hand on his chin.

"Not quite; the evidence does not add up. It took me some time to figure it out. The letter stated an 'honorable discharge.' However, in order for a discharge to take place, I have to go before a court martial hearing. Until then, I am missing in action. Sloppy work if you ask me, Rajesh, for someone who is so... educated? I'm surprised you didn't do a better job."

"It sounds like you thought of everything." With his forefinger covering his mouth, Rajesh's panther-like eyes stared Ali down from the opposite side of the wooden table.

"Not quite. There is one more thing. I'm certain you had something to do with the opium operation as well. And all the deaths the tabloids mentioned. Since opium comes from the fluid of the poppy plant, someone had to harvest it, and ship it across the sea. The only person who has knowledge of that is you. All the evidence points to you. So how did you get it, Rajesh? Are you running an operation in Kolachi, too?"

"How did you gather that?" the larger man inquired.

"You are the only one who could have brought the powder here. And what's worse, you involved my wife. An innocent in the matter."

"Bravo, Raza. I didn't think you'd be able to figure it out," Rajesh mocked as he applauded

"Although, I have to wonder…why?" Ali's eyes were shooting daggers.

"Have you grown an attraction to the girl?" Rajesh retorted.

"That's none of your concern; leave her out of this." A growl escaped from Ali.

"You are the one who mentioned her, Raza." Rajesh's gestured his hand into the air. "There would be no other reason why you would be…sheltering her."

"So, she doesn't become a victim of circumstance." As an answer to the question.

"Circumstance indeed. I do admit it was a clever scheme marrying her, to prevent deportation." A smirk tugged at Rajesh's lips.

"How do you know about that?" The answer clipped out faster than Ali could think.

"It is amazing what spies can find out."

"Jasper and Oliver. Of course," Ali muttered under his breath. "You've been following us all this time. That's how you sent the threats. So I would be sent to jail, and blamed for your crimes."

"Nothing gets by you," Rajesh mocked once again as he gave shrug as compliance.

"Then, what of the files, Rajesh?" Ali began again. "You remember those, too?"

"You saw that little trick, did you?" Ali's former friend asked. "I couldn't be responsible for the entire crime. Someone had to be the scapegoat."

"By the way, they're on their way to Moshin," Ali finished the sentence.

"Why, Ali Raza? Why, after all this time? We have fought side by side, as comrades, against the enemy, we were a team. We can do it again as a team. Why do you always go against me so?"

"Once again, Rajesh, don't be coy. You know very well that people are driven by fear. Their hate. If rich men have a hefty deal waved in front of their faces, they will succumb to any conditions. For instance, the land, our land. Especially if a profit can be gained; you would indulge them, even if it means not sullying your hands. The battle in the Thar was just a folly, entertainment to you, to satisfy your bloodlust." Silence filled the air between the two men. Ali was the first to break. "You have gone too far, Rajesh. You sabotage me, threaten my wife. Murder hundreds of innocent people. Do you have any idea what you have done?" Ali seethed.

"Nonetheless, we all know the outcome. The battle was a draw. But, it wasn't over for me. Not in the Thar, not here," Rajesh continued for him.

"What are you saying?" Ali's tone lowered at the statement.

"You can't be so inept, Raza," Rajesh berated. "If you had died in action there would have been no qualms; the title of First Lieutenant would have been bestowed on me. But you stole from me what was owed me—"

"Is this what it's about? Your entitlement?" Ali curtailed his sentence. "A title bestowed upon who is worthy, Rajesh, you know that more than anyone."

"My hatred for you is justifiable. For too long, you have taken what's rightfully mine. You are nothing but a lowly street dog, unworthy of a respectable rank in the military. I left you the dagger so you could end your life yourself, in a respectable manner." Ali could see his comrade's face contort in the dim light.

"And after you're done with all this madness? What will happen when you're satisfied with your revenge?" the hero protested.

"I will collect my earnings, and be gone from this flea-ridden place. And you—" Rajesh chuckled to himself. "You will die a beggar's death."

"The army will hunt you down to the ends of the earth once they find out the truth. You have disrespected yourself, your family, and your position. There is no hiding anymore, Rajesh." Ali tried to sway the militant man's mind.

To no avail, it only seemed to infuriate the man further. "Enough! I don't explain myself to anyone, least of all you. In a way, I am glad that you didn't waste away in that hellish wasteland. Because, now, I will have the satisfaction of killing you with my bare hands." With that statement, Rajesh lunged forward. Ali blocked his attack in time, catapulting the taller man into a pillar. Rajesh held

179

onto the wooden beam for support, and after a few moments he regained his balance.

The man shot forth like a bullet for a second attempt to attack Ali. With his hands out, Ali blocked the oncoming attack. Although, the larger man gained the upper hand; with one fell swoop, Rajesh pulled Ali's arms behind his back. With a free hand the muscular arm wrapped around the neck of Ali.

As he struggled to break free from the choke hold, Ali could hear his adversary's muffled voice in his ear. "You always did talk too much. I will relish stealing every last breath from your body."

Through the pain, Ali gained an advantage. While Rajesh was distracted Ali shifted his stance, and kicked the balance right out from the man, sending him straight to the wooden floor. As he caught his breath, Ali placed a hand to his throat to steady his breathing. "This is over, Rajesh; give it up."

"It will never be over until I'm rid of you." Panting, he picked himself up from the dusty floor.

Rajesh, like a mad tiger, continued to come for his prey. The two were matched in sparring skills. Back and forth, they threw punches and parried, until the two military officers grew weary. Then Rajesh gripped Ali's arm backwards, and administered an elbow punch to his spine, driving Ali to his knees. Ali used every ounce in his weary body to continue, but failed to summon the strength. Once again, Rajesh seized the opportunity, placing his muscular forearms in a death-lock. Ali found Rajesh's grip was too strong to break; he could feel unconsciousness taking over and he could hear his neck pop. Ali was weakening fast.

"Let me make it clear to you before you die. No matter what you say, no matter what you do, you will always be inferior. And that is the way it will always be!" Rajesh shouted at the unconscious man. Then, a whistle rang through the air between the two men, tearing flesh from Rajesh's cheek, and pierced the wall behind them, interrupting the scuffle.

"What?" a befuddled Rajesh murmured, and abruptly loosened his grip, which sent Ali to the floor in a choking fit. In an effort to regain air, Ali caught himself with a swift movement to prevent falling. When he looked up to see where Rajesh had gone, Ali could see that the foe set his sights on Charmaine, who perched herself on a suspended catwalk above them, holding a smoking gun. From a distance, he could tell her body shook from the adrenaline.

"You almost shot me!" Ali bellowed from across the room.

"I have only shot a gun one time before! You are very lucky that wasn't your head," Charmaine shouted back at him.

Then, chills wracked Ali's entire body. From the distance, he could see Charmaine's expression. Paralyzing fear. He had seen that expression on the faces of many men before they died. Now he saw it on her as Rajesh began to stride in her direction. "*Chinaal…*" Ali heard the words hiss out. And Charmaine struggled to escape her perch as Rajesh came dangerously close to her.

Ali knew he had to think fast. It was then he spotted a mallet on one of the old shipping crates. In the blink of an eye, he reached the crate and curled his fingers around the cool wood. In an instant Ali lifted the weight in his right hand, moved his arm in a backward motion and. with his remaining strength, flung the mallet in his opponent's direction. The heavy object hit its target, in the back of the knee, knocking Rajesh off balance. A yowl of pain escaped the injured man as he tumbled down the aged staircase. This allowed Charmaine the opportunity to escape.

It was now Ali's turn to react, and fear replaced aggression. With a reckless care, he reached the bottom of the staircase where Rajesh lay helpless; this was Ali's golden opportunity to strike. With a second rush of strength Ali rolled the brawny man over, encircled his forearms his neck. It was Ali's turn to hear the bones in Rajesh's neck crack. He was seconds away from total satisfaction.

"Your thought's kill you, don't they, Ali Raza?" Rajesh managed to choke out. "…You know you have to kill me. Revert to that side…Your dark side…But we both know…you are a spineless coward." Sputtering, spittle oozing from his mouth, Rajesh continued to taunt his opponent. "How do you think…you can kill a monster; without becoming one yourself?" A soft, ragged chuckle escaped his lips.

"ALI! Don't give in to your hatred. That's what he wants." Those words struck a chord with him. *Ali*...his name echoed in his ears. All his life he'd never wanted to kill, only to defend himself. But never by choice. He hated the dark side. He had done everything necessary to keep it in check. Now had it come it down to. *Can I?* The gasping sounds from Rajesh jerked Ali from his thoughts, prompting him to release the death-hold he had on him.

With a loud *thud,* Rajesh collapsed to the floor, and a plume of dust rose around them. Ali stood stoic for long moments, comprehending the situation that transpired. Finally, he lifted his head to see Charmaine take a breath of relief. Descending the steel stairs, she sailed into his arms. Catching her with crushing admiration, he buried his face in her hair, savoring the moment. Ali had never been more relieved and angry all at once. "What are you doing here? How did you find me? Didn't I tell you not to interfere? Don't you know you could have gotten yourself killed?" Just as shaken as she, he smoothed her hair away from her face.

"You knew I wouldn't listen. I couldn't let you do this alone. And speaking of getting oneself killed...who leaves without a trace? Without as much as a goodbye?"

"I did say so, it's just that you weren't awake," Ali stated as he flashed her his devilish smirk. His wife gave him a quizzical look. She opened her mouth to speak once again, when a familiar voice cut in.

"How quaint." Charmaine blanched at the sound of a gun cocked into place.

"Henrietta…" Ali spoke, acknowledging Henrietta Flint's presence. "How nice of you to join us." Charmaine turned to face the elder woman as the loaded pistol was aimed at the couple. "Hands up where I can see them. Come now, the both of you. Now you, give me your gun." Ali obeyed the command, and he set his holstered semiautomatic pistol it on the floor and kicked it in Henrietta's direction. Henrietta circled around them, and picked up the discarded weapon. "You two caused me a lot of trouble, you know. Because of you…because of this odious girl."

"Me?" Charmaine gave a coy response.

"Well, not entirely. Since the night you discovered my scheme with the opium, we have been busy searching for you, and this caused a delay in business. Not to mention Jasper and Oliver's idiocy, when they found your nefarious man at the Stag. Those two blithering imbeciles confessed to everything. The entire scheme." Henrietta waved the gun in the air. "The police came and raided my shop; now I'm left with nothing. My reputation is further tarnished because of you. And now you will have nothing."

"Henrietta. I don't understand…Why?" Charmaine managed to choke out.

"We'll skip the details. Let's just say one ruination after another will change a woman. No worries, however, as I've learned my lesson the hard way," the shop-owner confirmed.

"And what was that?" Ali challenged.

"Be conniving in every deed. Give no mercy and have no remorse."

"No, that's not true. Just because you're dealt a bad hand doesn't mean you should be bitter or spiteful." Charmaine's subconscious clicked to her mother.

"No, perhaps not. But, like I said before. This is a man's world. And nothing we can do can change that."

"What I don't understand is how you and Rajesh found each other," Ali interjected.

"You should know that one, Mr. Raza. The underground is where I found him. He was in need of disposing of his stock. And I was in need of keeping my business afloat, at least for a little while. So, we struck a deal. You know the rest. Now, all that's left is to finish with you two. On second thought, I could take the girl with me. Her services could be useful. We'll jump ship. I'm thinking, maybe a life in my beloved France. We'll sell what's left of the opium. Then more victims will come pouring in."

"Over my dead body," Charmaine retorted.

"Have it your way. Move. Outside," Henrietta responded in a calm manner. As the group began the trek to the door, a dark figure rose from the shadows.

"Nooo!" A loud snarl escaped the injured Rajesh. He was hell-bound and determined to wrestle the gun from Henrietta, having no intention of dying by her hand.

Pitink! Pitink! Shots ricocheted off the walls as Ali shielded Charmaine from the onslaught as they raced to the door. In a low growl, Ali clutched his arm in pain. Charmaine turned to see what happened; she opened her mouth to say something, until Ali cut her off.

"Go!" he shouted.

"I can't leave you like this," Charmaine protested.

"You can and you will. I cannot risk you being injured," Ali countered as he shoved her through the door.

When he could see that she was safe, he turned to the scene playing before him. Rajesh and Henrietta were wrestling for the gun. He could feel the warm blood trickle down his arm; it didn't stop him, though. Ali dove, somersaulting for the weapon. Gripping the cool steel in his hands, he tested it.

Click! Click! Damn. The barrel was empty. He patted his side, then remembered.

When silence encompassed the building, Rajesh and Henrietta finished their kerfuffle and saw Ali holding the pistol in his one good hand, aimed directly at the duo.

"Do you really intend to shoot me with that, Raza? It's out of bullets." Rajesh inched little by little.

Ali called his bluff, and shot a bullet into the floor. "Think again." Rajesh promptly lifted his hands slowly, and Henrietta followed suit.

I need a little more time. "This is over, Rajesh. Just accept it," Ali announced.

"You haven't won yet, Raza," Rajesh retorted.

"Then I will end it," Ali gave a dangerous reply.

Aiming point blank at Rajesh, Ali cocked the pistol...

"Drop your weapons!" Whistling noises filled the air and a brigade of armed officers surrounded the trio. Ali cocked his head in the direction of the squadron and dropped his gun. Moments later, the constable walked through the door.

"Well, look what we have here, Henrietta Flint," the officer spoke. "We've been tracking you for months. When we raided the shop, we found no trace of you. We assumed you'd disappeared, until now." The constable turned his attentions to Rajesh. "And this one must be Rajesh Suneel, opium dealer. The Indian government informed us you might be here. Although it seemed farfetched."

"I suspect we have you to thank in apprehending the criminals, Mr. Raza?" the officer asked.

"Yes, sir," Ali acknowledged.

"Well done. We'll notify your superior officers of this heroic deed." Ali nodded in acceptance.

Ali followed the police officers as they escorted Rajesh and Henrietta from the warehouse in handcuffs.

Upon exiting the building, he could see Charmaine sprinting in his direction. As she sailed into his arms, Ali winced in pain. Then he wrapped his good arm around her and instantly relaxed.

"Your arm!" Charmaine announced as she released from his embrace.

"It's nothing," Ali countered.

"Your wound needs attention," his wife insisted.

"I've been in worse situations," Ali proclaimed.

However, Charmaine wouldn't hear anymore. "Now listen here. I will not hear any more arguments, mister; you will have that arm looked at whether you like it or not…" She wasn't able to finish her sentence, as a familiar voice called her name.

"Charmaine, Charmaine! Oh, my dear girl…" Arthur Radcliffe released a chuckle of relief.

"Papa, Papa!" Charmaine instantly ran for her father.

"Thank heavens you're safe," he exclaimed.

"It's such relief to see you. How did you find us?" Charmaine questioned.

"The Yard alerted me of your location. When I heard, I rushed here as soon as I got the news," Arthur answered.

"Who alerted the police?" she asked.

"I did." Ali cleared his throat from behind. "When I left the house this morning I went to the police station with a note, directing them to the warehouse. I didn't know if I would make it back safely. So, I had the police call upon your father. To make sure you were safe, if something were to happen to me."

"And you are?" Arthur Radcliffe questioned.

"Lt. Ali Raza, sir," Ali answered the father.

"My husband, Papa," Charmaine forced out.

"Pardon? I don't think I heard…correctly….I think you need to tell me the entire story."

"Gladly. But for now, we need to tend to your son-in-law's wound." Looping her hand through her father's arm, they all walked home.

Chapter 22

"I see," Arthur Radcliffe pondered as he stared out the bay window. "That is quite a story indeed."

They were all situated in the parlor of the Radcliff home. Charmaine and Ali sat in the plum- colored Victorian wingback chairs.

"Papa?" Charmaine waited for a response.

"I could never imagine Henrietta Flint would become such a villain." Arthur turned from the window to face Charmaine and Ali.

"Your mother often spoke of Henrietta. Although, not in the manner you had described." The perplexed father shook his head side to side to banish the thoughts from his head, then turned to face them. "When she attained the money from her divorce, her shop grew. But, rumors spread of her progress, as well as her reputation. Soon, no one would buy from a business woman whose reputation was tainted. It was only a matter of time before the income of the business became tight," Charmaine continued.

"That is when she found Rajesh, who needed to disperse the opium he brought over from India," Ali continued for her.

"Her marriage to Eric Flint was not exactly the

most the ideal," Arthur pointed out.

"But all that is behind us. Now, let us focus on the future ahead of us. And it seems I owe you a debt of gratitude, Lt. Raza, for rescuing my daughter," Arthur breathed out.

"Thank you, sir." Ali nodded. "Now, I have something for you," he continued as he rose from the chair. Ali took a turn around the room, both Charmaine and Arthur eyeing him bewilderedly.

"There is a matter I would like to address regarding your company, Mr. Radcliff," Ali continued with his statement. "A short time ago, a business investment was made between one William Tate and yourself. Unfortunately, the investment fell through and the culprit made a break for it. Never to be heard from again."

"We know the story; what's the point?" Arthur shot back.

"The point is Tate is now apprehended. It seems he left a string of broken hearts as well as empty pocketbooks around the country. I happened to come across this information while tracking down Rajesh. I saw the Radcliffe name on one of the files back at the records department. The thought hadn't occurred to me until Charmaine said something when we were in…"

"Hiding," Charmaine finished his sentence. Pink stained her cheeks.

"Yes. With that said, your business, along with all your losses, will be reimbursed."

"Darling, are you completely serious?" Charmaine spoke as she rose from her chair.

"Of course. Which brings me to my next point. India has substantial history, as well as holdings, with England. With my connections, I have contacted one of my companions who would be able to help you rebuild what you have lost." Ali turned back to them, both agape.

"You should receive a telegram from him within a few months."

Charmaine hastened to his side. She took his face between her hands and kissed him with glee. Only to break it when Arthur cleared his throat. A hint of red crossed her cheeks when she turned away.

"It seems I am indebted to you yet again…"

"There is no need. What happened to you and Charmaine should never have happened. And because of Charmaine, my name is redeemed. It is I who owe you."

"Name anything you want, and it is yours."

"I want nothing; only your blessing," Ali said with slow confidence. Arthur struck a match, lighting the tobacco in the bowl of his pipe, contemplating. He waved the stick in the air a few times before speaking again.

"It is most unusual."

"Papa, really, after all he has done you can't think to refuse…"

"I haven't agreed or disagreed with anything, yet. I am simply…comprehending a great deal on the matter. Somewhere along the way, you grew. But, the fact remains that you are married. And…I have no say in the matter. As a parent, one faces many challenges; one of those is accepting that fact." Arthur placed a soft kiss on his daughter's forehead.

"Papa."

Arthur Radcliffe turned to face his son-in-law. "Lt. Ali Raza, you have my blessing."

~*~*~

As the voices drifted through the parlor, Charmaine slipped from their sight. She ascended the creaking stairs to her bedroom for the first time in months. With her hand on the silver knob, she gave the white door a gentle push. Peering inside the empty room, everything in the silent room remained as it was before. The faint smell of lavender wafted through the room. And the shawl that she had worn that morning was draped on the foot of bed. Charmaine crossed the hardwood floor, her hand gliding across the cool, white iron frame of her bed. Her eyes caught sight of the writing desk.

With fingertips in between the gap, Charmaine gave the shutter a forceful push. Stray papers were scattered throughout, along with ink pens and other memorabilia. Among the debris, a black journal lay covered in a light layer of dust. Flipping through the pages, Charmaine grazed the pencil marks on the aged paper. The paper had begun to discolor. She clutched the book to her chest, then froze when the stack of letters in the corner caught her attention. Charmaine hesitated for a moment before placing the book down to reach for the stack. The color of the paper on the envelope had turned, as had the paper in the design book.

Charmaine unwrapped the black ribbon that held the stack together. Her finger slid across the brittle paper and tore open an envelope. The room began to fill with warmth once again as Charmaine began reading her mothers' letter.

April 26, 1905
To my darling Daughter,

~Epilogue~

Six Months Later

The sky was painted brilliant colors of reds and pinks, mixed with clear blue. On the docks of London port, the sound of boots resounded on the old wood dock. General Moshine Sher and Ali made their way to the pier as a ship carried exported the last of cargo to the Sub-Continent.

"It seems congratulations are in order, Lieutenant. When we hadn't seen or heard anything for months, we thought the worst." The superior officer spoke with respect. "I could hardly believe my eyes when your letter came, along with the forged documents as evidence. We had no idea an officer with such high esteem such as second Lieutenant Suneel could be responsible for such an act. He will return to Delhi, where he'll serve a ten-year sentence for his crimes."

"To be honest," Ali began, "I couldn't have done it without help." He turned in Charmaine's direction, beaming with pride.

"After all that has happened, there are not enough words for a formal apology. I only hope that you accept my gratitude and apology, Lieutenant."

"I only wish I could do more, General."

"Actually, there is something you can do. There is a position opening for Captain. The position is yours if you want to accept it."

"I don't know what to say," Ali responded.

"Say yes. You deserve it. With all you have done, it's only right." That was the first time Ali had heard his friend speak in such high honor of him.

"I'm going to need some time to think this over, but you will have an answer." Ali gave the general's offer a dignified response.

"Excellent. I await your answer by the end of the year." The superior officer acknowledged the answer with a quick nod.

"You will have it, sir." Ali gave his reassurance to his friend.

The two men faced one another as they clasped hands and shook in agreement. They turned in unison at the sound of Rajesh's voice shouting:

"Don't think for one second that these chains will stop me, Raza! You won't get away with this! I will see you and yours dead! You will be sure to count on that." General Sher gave a salute as he turned on his heel towards his ship.

Ali watched for a few minutes before the superior officer disappeared from sight. He strolled to the street where his chestnut horse waited with his groom. Judging by the way the horse bobbed his head up and down, the horse grew restless. Ali patted and smoothed his neck to calm his friend. He turned away to stare at the ocean ahead of him.

The light sound of footsteps broke his reverie. He turned to find Charmaine and her father, arm in arm, strolling in his direction. Ali couldn't help but sneak a small smile as she approached. His wife looked rather fetching in a red and white pinstripe day dress, a red sash tied about her waist, and a white, wide-brimmed feathered hat atop her neat, coiffured hair. Her delicate hand griped a white parasol, which protected her from the afternoon sun. She looked every inch of perfection.

"What was that Mr. Suneel was shouting, darling?" Charmaine inquired in a sweet voice.

"Only cursing our name and announcing his revenge on us all." Ali gave a smug smile.

"You are not amusing, darling," his wife countered.

"Had to lighten the mood somehow." Ali gave a smug smile.

"A rather strange way, don't you think?" Arthur Radcliffe pointed out.

"Oh, think nothing of it, Papa; Ali was teasing." Charmaine gave a slight tap on her father's arm to gain his attention.

"Yes, well, here's one for lightening up the mood," Arthur began. "Since my recent development with Mr. Babur and his trade, my business has tripled. With enough silks, spices, fine jewelry, and pottery he has provided us, we are able to rebuild.

"And with the materials provided, the bank has approved us for a loan. I plan to buy back Henrietta's shop. I've already hired men to remodel the building. We should be in business by the end of spring."

"Papa…" Charmaine replied with shock.

"And all thanks to you, my boy," Arthur Radcliffe expressed with gratitude.

"No thanks necessary. My only reward is seeing you both successful." Arthur took Ali's hand in his for a firm handshake. The sound of a horse's grunt of approval was also heard as Arthur Radcliffe and the couple strolled from the docks to the shore, where a groom held the reins of the chestnut gelding.

"Say, darling, isn't that Henrietta's horse?" Charmaine asked.

"Why, yes, it is. I adopted the poor boy," Ali replied. "His name is *Azzadi*."

"*Azzadi*?" Charmaine questioned.

"It means 'Freedom.' I thought it fitting with what we've been through." Ali turned to the large animal, and stroked his neck.

"Where do you intend to keep him?" his wife inquired, rather perplexed.

"At the stable, of course. I figured he could use a good home." Azzadi gave his reply with a head butt into Ali's shoulder; it was the creature's way of asking for more attention. Which Ali acknowledged with another stroke on its neck.

"Ahh, would you mind, Papa, if I had a moment alone with my husband?" Charmaine turned away from Ali to ask her father.

"Of course, my dear. If you will excuse me." Arthur released his arm from its hold. Charmaine drew Ali aside to walk on the opposite side pier.

Ali offered his arm to Charmaine, which she accepted. As the couple strolled the docks, his wife noticed his apprehension. "You seem troubled, darling. Do you mind telling me what the matter is?"

"My superior officer offered me a promotion." Ali lifted his head as he stared straight into the distance, his ebony locks blowing in the light breeze.

"That's wonderful news," Charmaine responded, her tone solemn. She knew what that might mean. Her heart lurched at the thought of Ali leaving.

"Although, I am uncertain if they will station me in India. I can petition to work in an office here. The military tends to be strict on certain policies."

"Since you are a hero now, I am sure they won't mind if you have a watchful eye for any suspicious activity in the city," Charmaine pointed out. She turned to hear his response. What she saw was his face, void of expression. It seemed as if ages passed before one of them would speak. The roar of the ocean waves crashing into shore drew him back to reality.

"I almost did it, *Jaan*. I almost killed him; I almost killed Rajesh out of anger, out of hatred, something I vowed I would never do. I have been so blinded by my lust for revenge, I failed to see what I needed was peace. I don't know what I would have done if you were not there." Ali turned away from her to speak. "If something like that happens again, I may not be able to control myself."

Charmaine placed a hand on his cheek; Ali turned to face her. "Don't say that, darling. No matter what Rajesh said, you are not a monster. You have proven that time and again," she comforted.

"It seems as if you are the only one who can calm the rage within me," Ali uttered as he took her hand in his and brought it to his lips.

"You did that before I came," Charmaine spoke in a humble manner.

"Not the way you can. Before you came into my life, I had so many sins on my shoulders. Sins I can't redeem. But when you are by my side I have the courage to face what comes to me." Charmaine noticed Ali tense up at the statement.

"We all have past sins we can't make up for. That doesn't define us." Charmaine gave a slight brush of her hand in a soft stroke across Ali's face.

"You're always the optimist. I wish more than anything that could be true." Ali nudged his head to meet her hand.

"Darling, this may not be important now," Charmaine intervened to change the subject. "But, do you remember, when you asked me to describe, in detail, what happened that night of my abduction? Well, there was one thing I forgot to mention."

"What was that?" Ali queried.

"Henrietta. She wanted me to join her in her opium scheme. I refused, of course." Charmaine had waited ages to confess that piece of information.

"Thank heavens you did." Ali gave her admiration. "I don't want to think about what would have happened if you accepted. You could have caused an even bigger scandal than what we have already created." Her husband pulled Charmaine closer to his hard chest. Charmaine trailed her hands up to the collar of his shirt, and toyed with it.

"Like to think of the sinful charade we caused in the alley? For example." Charmaine gave a sly smile.

"And the library," Ali chimed in. "Can you forgive me for turning you into a wanton, thus creating such scandal?"

"Oh, I may hold you accountable." Charmaine gave a teasing smile.

"I have the notion you plan on driving me crazy for the rest of my life," Ali suggested.

"That. Plus, I do have that red dress you love" A smile broadened across the impish girl's face.

"You wench." Ali gave a bold chuckle.

"By the way, what made you finally change your mind about how you felt about me?" Charmaine finally asked.

"Myra, the tavern woman." Ali's answer was curt.

"Excuse me?" Charmaine's eyebrows quirked at the response.

"It's not how it sounds. Upon my arrest, I was…disoriented," Ali explained.

"I remember." Charmaine repulsed at the answer.

"I…ahh…sort of told her, Myra, about you; that I was in love with you. And she told me to follow how I felt, and to hell with the rules. Or something like that."

"Is it still true? Do you still fancy yourself in love with me?" Charmaine shivered in preparation of the answer.

"Without a doubt," Ali whispered against her lips.

"Well, then, I must thank her." Charmaine pulled her husband in for a kiss.

The End.

Acknowledgments

First of all, I would like to thank everyone, who have lent their support to me while on this path of writing. Who continued to believe in me, and cheer me on through this whole endeavor. To my friends: Isabelle G., Samantha, R., Jessica B, Karen S., and Leigh L.

My Family: Aunt Shelley, my Mom Christine, Grandma Cindy, and Donna J. Thank you for being my cheerleaders when I wanted to give up.

My Critique Partners: Madeline M, who is detail oriented. For that I am thankful. Karen S. Thank you for understanding me.

As well as my book coach Sue Barnett, who encouraged me to do my best in writing. I don't know how to thank you all enough.

A special, heart-felt thank you to my editor Kim Huther.

Did you know?

Women like Charmaine, although (she was) educated at the time of her youth, had very limited education? The women in 1910, regardless of class background, were seen as second class citizens - a right denied them due parliamentary vote. Since childhood, women were encouraged to serve others, to consider the interests of their husbands, fathers and brothers first rather than their own. Thus, limiting their chances of a good future.

When she did work. The second class working woman found a job in the clothing industry, and paid very poorly, less than 65 pounds a year. ($85 in American standards).

Women had to scrimp, save and pawn most of their things to survive. Like Charmaine, she had to pawn many of her dresses just to make ends meet.

If women were educated. Their education was very limited in geography and history. Less focused on the three R's: Reading, Writing & Arithmetic. And a large portion to domestic work. Such as: needle work, house work, childcare, household management and cookery.

If you are interested, and want to learn more: http://www.mirror.co.uk/news/uk-news/everywoman-1910-no-vote-poor-206289

Secondly, the Kindjal Dagger that Ali uncovers clues on, is an actual weapon. It was created in 1850 by the Ottomans. I used it in the story because it had so much history.

The book Charmaine & Ali found at the London Public Library is an actual book? Although the Dagger might not be in the book. I modified it a bit to fit the story. The book however, may not be at the actual public library:

It is 485 paged equipped with battle plans, 4 fold out maps and it is for sale! – For Eighty-five pounds that is.

The Decisive Battles of India: 1746-1849 by G. B. [George Bruce] Malleson. First published in 1883 by W.H.

Allen Co.

Furthermore, did you know? That India & Pakistan were all one country during the Edwardian Era. Ali, although his family lives in Kolachi, (modern day Karachi, Pakistan) his family has origins in the Gujrat regions of India.

It wasn't until 1947, when Britain finally left the region. That the Muslims wanted their own independence. Though Ali's family was Muslim, there is such a thing as "Indian Muslims," during that time. He fell out of faith because of all the crimes that had happened in his country. Especially to his family.

On a final note. In old countries, such as India. It is customary, that the younger generation addresses the elders as "Uncle", "Aunti", or "Sir". If they are not their parents. It is considered disrespectful without such. That is why Ali refers to Mehdi as "Uncle." Out of respect.

Made in the USA
Lexington, KY
24 November 2018